Out of Business

Simon Pearce

ISBN:
978-1-9160503-7-2

Copyright © 2021 by Simon Pearce

Published by

Space Monkey
Creations Ltd

www.spacemonkeycreations.com

Part 3
of
The Business Trilogy

Chapter 1 – Present

The Atom Café

The narrow alley, lined with piss-stained brick walls between empty glass doors and windows with white frames, stretched out before him like some weird reflection in a funhouse mirror. The close graffiti-covered walls to either side looked like they were about to squeeze in against his slim frame and crush his feeble-looking shoulders. It reminded Toby of a dolly zoom in a movie, also known as a push-pull if he remembered correctly, mimicking the kind of sensation people appeared to experience when having a bout of vertigo. Of course, this strange and giddy sensation and its setting were all part and parcel of living where he lived now, as was the stale smell of semen and bleach.

He'd had a long stint away from these kinds of effects on his mental faculties and five senses, but now he was back at it again on a daily basis with no time off or breaks back to reality. No, now he could indulge in as much as he wanted as often as he wanted. And he wanted as much as he could get his dirty digits on. For years he had cooked and consumed industrial levels of hard drugs, and as a result he'd been sent to prison where the quality of gear had been strong for the average fiend but far below par for a connoisseur like himself. When his sentence was served he'd had to suffice with whatever was available when he was back on the streets, merely scraping by on regular bud and common quality cocaine while working, running and hiding out as an outlaw. The moniker suited his outward appearance. His blond hair was long and unkept, as was his beard. He hadn't had a haircut or shave in years now and had an obscure heroin-junkie Viking appearance. Not something most people were used to seeing, including Toby when he looked at his reflection in the curtained windows he strolled past. Inside though he didn't feel like an outlaw. Sure he thought it sounded cool in some nerdy romanticised way, but in reality he didn't feel like he was breaking any laws. He was still just a cook, not a proper dangerous criminal.

At night these neon-lit doors he walked past were occupied by the gorgeous and talented sex workers of the infamous De Wallen, better known as Amsterdam's Red Light district. The hookers didn't care what Toby looked like – as long as he had the funds they'd fuck him. They'd fuck and even pretend to enjoy it, pretend to fancy you, pretend you were hung like a thoroughbred race horse with the physique of a golden Adonis. These days it was rare that Toby bothered to indulge in physical pleasures, preferring instead to experience the psychological and psychedelic kinds. For him busting a nut was all well and good, but travelling between dimensions and speaking to Gaia was far more worthy a pursuit and better use of his time. On rare occasions he would stroll these alleys at night along with the other hound dogs, staring at the flesh on display until you saw the shape and hue of something you fancied. But there was nothing to see at this time of day in the glass windows. No bikini clad-bodies or red lights, or even blue lights if he-shes were what you were into, just the first purple rays of sunlight heralding a new day and the obese figure of Femke, one of the cleaners who worked the alleys at this ungodly hour wiping the tiles and scrubbing the stains from the night before.

On a few occasions when Toby had first started working here, he had stopped and talked to Femke. It had started because he was off his face after staying awake on another lengthy binge of shrooms and shards when he mistook her for one of the inter-dimensional beings he often encountered when playing with his usual poison of dimethyltryptamine, better known as DMT. Toby had followed her into one of the small rooms and, much to her shock, given her a giant bear hug while informing her how pleased he was to see her trying to clean up the Red Light district. At that time, he had taken it as a sign that Mother Earth was in full support of prostitution. Luckily for Toby, Femke had a healthy sense of humour and was used to the stragglers from the night before still wandering De Wallen and acting strange because of whatever they'd flooded their systems with.

There were a few occasions after that when Toby would stop to chat over a cup of coffee with the cleaner, but now most mornings they would simply give each other a friendly smile and wave while continuing about their business in the heart of Amsterdam's main tourist zone. Toby couldn't understand how Femke could be so cheerful at such an hour, let alone while cleaning the cum of a thousand cocks from the tiles of the whores' rooms. The men were like animals at night in De Wallen, all clamouring over one another like rabid rats to get a view of the flesh or jeer abuse at some other random beast who stalked the alleys and canal ways. The mess they left for Femke to clean was incredible.

Between the narrow alleys that almost felt like a straitjacket tightening around his unwashed frame, he pulled his filthy coat in around him to stop the bite of the chill drifting up from the canals. Even in spring the cold from the water's surface was uncomfortable for Toby's wiry, malnourished body. As he hurried over one of the humped cobbled bridges a breeze hit him and sent a shiver down his spine, causing him to sober up a little from the hit he'd smoked before leaving the flat to go to work. He forced his legs to carry him quicker to his destination, where he knew there was a plentiful supply of all manner of narcotics waiting for him to consume.

As he made it to the end of the final alley on the other side of De Wallen he fished the keys out of his pocket and approached the wooden door of the corner building. He unlocked the entrance and stepped inside, directly below the sign bearing the name: The Atom Café.

The coffee shop was situated right on the edge of De Wallen on a corner that gave its floor-to-ceiling windows a fantastic panorama-like view of all the comings and goings of the densely populated tourist spot. The metal barriers that protruded from the narrow roads leading into the Red Light district could be seen from the café's window. If it wasn't for all of the pungent skunk and sweet hashish being smoked in the coffee shop over the course of a regular day, you'd be able to smell the sex and body lotions of the prostitute's neon cubicles.

Some nights Toby could smell the sex on his customers. The location of the café meant that they regularly had tourists stumbling directly from beneath the red lights into the shadows of the shop. A mezzanine area overlooking the ground floor, as well as the wooden staircase leading up to it, meant that there were plenty of places to sit in darkness away from prying eyes to enjoy your high and not ruin your buzz. Many of the smokers who frequented Toby's place were not ready for the strength of his gear, which meant the dark corners to hide in and suffer the paranoia in peace were very welcome indeed. Toby would regularly peer into the gloom to see nervous, half-closed eyes squinting back at him. Another tourist unsure of whether or not they would make it back to their hotel or hostel safely, not knowing if that feeling in their gut would soon make an unscheduled appearance all over the scarred pine table before them. That was one of the few negative aspects about running a coffee shop in Amsterdam for Toby – the vomit. If he spotted them soon enough, he could supply them with the necessary sugar-filled and vitamin-packed beverage to prevent any projectile puke from occurring. But he wasn't always on point himself due to the vast quantities of drugs he was now consuming on an hourly basis.

Toby had now reached a point where just getting out of bed in the morning required a hit of meth or fat line of Charlie. Fortunately for him, there was always a plentiful supply of both kept on standby on the cabinet next to his single bed. After the appropriate dosage of whatever rocket fuel he consumed for breakfast had been ingested, a big fat spliff of Kryptonite was usually smoked in order to allow the first drug to properly work its magic. Then a giant mug of coffee with another spliff before heading out into the daylight to open up the café for another day of supplying tourists – and the locals who knew best – with the finest quality cannabis in all of Europe, possibly even the world.

As he gave the wooden furnishings a quick wipe down, he smoked a small spliff of his latest sativa. Toby hadn't named it yet, but due to its zesty tang he knew that a fruit-orientated name was in order. The christening could wait, what was more important for a professional like Toby was the head. If it didn't meet his high standards then it was pointless naming it. He would just flog it on to some other coffee shop and let them call it whatever the fuck they liked. It tasted good and smoked well enough, but he wasn't sure about the potency yet. He considered the dilemma that he was still too wrecked from everything he'd had for breakfast and ended the previous night on to really judge the bud properly, but figured that as long as he just kept smoking the same strain all day then by the evening he'd know if it was a keeper or not; stoner logic of the highest order.

He made sure that the fridges were all stocked with sugary beverages, and that the colourful labels were all facing outward to entice the wasted customers, then placed some scrumptious looking cakes and cookies in the counter display before wiping the glass casing to prevent any idiots from not noticing the sign informing them of the THC dosage in his sweet treats. On more than one occasion some half-baked newbie in the Dam had not realised that they were buying space cake, cooked by Toby no less, and then wound up in need of medical attention. Toby always made his confectionery with doses strong enough for him to enjoy should he get peckish during the day, so of course the average Amsterdam visitor struggled with what they ate. In the beginning Toby had regularly warned people of how lethal they were, but then he got fed up with strangers acting like they could handle the same levels of THC that he could and looking down their noses at him for insinuating that the cakes were too much of a good thing. Now he tried to remember to clean the glass and left the rest to fate, science, karma, God or whatever else there was to prevent young stoners from collapsing in his coffee shop. While the authorities couldn't prosecute Toby for making the cakes so strong, they were getting tired of tourists slumped in nearby alleyways and needing medical attention because of them.

Once the coffee shop was stocked and cleaned ready for action he descended into the basement to get the other business up and running. Below the legitimate establishment, Toby had built an entirely new place of industry. Down here he cooked crank, crack and codeine. It had blown Toby away when the criminals he supplied informed him that the youth of today were using cough syrup to get fucked-up on, and that a shit-ton of cash could be made from manufacturing the stuff rather than boosting it from chemists and warehouses. Now, Toby sipped it like a glass of fine wine, savouring the flavour and swilling it around in his rancid mouth to check the quality of it. Toby was pretty sure it was the reason he was so sluggish when trying to get off his mattress most mornings.

He set to work on heating up the hot plates and setting out the Erlenmeyer flasks and various liquids ready to bring to a slow simmer, knowing that he'd probably be working alone all day today and would have to tend the counter at the coffee shop as well as maintain things in the basement if he was to stay on track for their next delivery. Once the chemicals and cookers were all at the appropriate temperatures to be left unsupervised without fear of burning the place down, Toby climbed a metal ladder that took him up past both floors of the coffee shop behind a thin wall until he reached the roof space.

There, he stepped off the ladder and onto the wooden flooring of the attic, which was surrounded by plastic sheeting hanging from the ceiling and illuminated by harsh metal halide and high-pressure sodium lights. He stripped and put his overalls on, which hung from a nail by the ladder. Toby then parted the plastic and stepped into his most favourite place in the world – his grow room. Just like his old house, Toby had converted the entire upper floor into a place to farm crops of the strongest buds he could cultivate. Kryptonite, along with several other strains, filled the large area and grew tall in the ample space provided by the coffee shop's lofty attic. He checked the water pumps and strength of the lights, ensured that all of the other levels were fine for optimum growth and then smiled as he went back out through the plastic sheets safe in the knowledge that his babies were all growing to be strong and healthy. They would be all they could be, and then some.

Back down on the ground floor of the coffee shop, Toby took one last look around to do a mental check of everything that needed doing and then nodded confirmation to himself that all was ready. He approached the entrance and turned the neon sign on that hung in the glass to show the world that The Atom Café was now ready to fuck you on all four fronts – buyer beware.

Days were pretty standard at the coffee shop. Serve the customers with whatever puff and drinks they wanted, while keeping an eye on the ones that looked like they would paint the floor and walls with their over consumption. Check the levels of stock to try and ensure that they never ran out of anything. Roll joints to sell to customers who couldn't or were too high to roll their own. And in between these regular duties he had to keep an eye on the illegal operations in the basement and attic. The bulk of the work that took place there had to be handled when he wasn't tending to the coffee shop customers, but there were days where Toby could get things done in preparation. Today was one of those days. The coffee shop had regular foot traffic, but wasn't particularly busy as the tourist season was yet to kick off properly. When there were minimal numbers of tokers in the joint he could slip up and down the ladder and check everything was running smoothly before reappearing from behind the counter. Toby figured that he didn't really have to worry about leaving the coffee shop unattended for these brief spells due to the fact that his clientele were all stoned or stoners patient enough to wait to get even more stoned; good people.

Over the course of the day he served the customers and kept the café ticking along without incident, all the while consuming as many drugs as he felt like. The coffee shop was almost as good as the house in the UK he'd been dealing from in terms of freedom to get fucked up. The only difference now was that he had to operate a cash register and serve drinks as well as narcotics. Otherwise, it was debauchery as usual for Toby. He chain-smoked spliffs, only one strain today for quality control reasons, as well as surreptitiously popping pills and snorting lines. After the sun had set, he began sipping syrup too, which helped mellow him out and bring him down on the days he'd get too carried away on the crank and coke.

The law stated that all coffee shops needed to close by 2.00 am at the absolute latest, so by around 1.30 Toby would begin ushering customers out and only serving people under the condition that they were buying to go. Stoners always took a while to get moving. Toby took it easy on them – he could relate, and so he would simply walk from table to table and casually instruct them to gather up their belongings and 'fuck off' – nothing too heavy-handed in his opinion.

On this particular evening The Atom Café emptied relatively quickly, mainly due to the lack of bodies to begin with, so by about five to two there was only the one customer left sitting at the back under the stairs. Toby moved from table to table, wiping them down with a damp cloth and pushing any debris into the small bin he carried with him.

"Time to fuck off," Toby slurred as he cleaned a table. "The shop's closed."

"This is my first time in Amsterdam," the customer stated matter-of-factly from the shadows. His voice was deep and had a thick Welsh accent. Toby recognised its timbre immediately but thought nothing of it.

"Hope you're having fun, but now you have to move that fun on to somewhere else mate." Toby finished wiping the tables and then set to clearing the counter. There were still a couple of cakes left, but the cookies had all sold. This made Toby smile, knowing just how strong his cookies were and that somewhere in the city tonight there would be tourists dropping out of reality as a multitude of waves came smashing into their psyche from all of the THC and other goodies he'd placed into his confectionary. He was pretty sure today's batch had only contained THC and very minute quantities of psilocybin, not like the DMT batches he'd sold in the past as a dangerous social experiment that seemed fine to him at the time, but he regretted later when hearing news of tourists freaking out and causing the trains to be stopped due to a lot of 'free love' being performed on the tracks, as well as hotel closures for a multitude of deviant acts being performed on their premises involving live animals and dead people.

"Fun?" the final customer queried from the shadows.

"Fun, business, pleasure, debauchery. Whatever you wanna call it, take it outside as I gotta lock up," Toby retorted without a second thought.

"Fun?" the stranger asked a second time. "No," he answered

his own question on this occasion. "Business?" he asked out loud, more to himself than Toby. "Too impersonal," again he answered his own question, which Toby wasn't even really listening to. "No, this is about something else," the customer said confidently, a slight raise in volume now that he was getting emotional about it. "This is definitely something personal. This is something that has taken me over water and across several countries." The man's voice continued to grow with emotion and intensity. Toby remained oblivious. "It's tested me physically, mentally and spiritually." The voice almost boomed godlike now.

"Don't tell me you lot have started invading coffee shops now!" Toby threw the cloth down onto the counter and looked up at the ceiling in despair.

"What?" The mystery man was now confused.

"Fucking Jehovah's Witnesses!" Toby blurted out as he dropped his head down and shook it in an attempt to suppress his anger at the thought of the Bible bashers intruding into his space yet again. "You know the last time I met any of your lot things didn't turn out well for them." His mind flashed back to that fateful evening when he was in an even more fucked-up state than he was tonight, where events had gone sideways and spiralled quickly downwards into mayhem when he had taken part in the murder of two unfortunate souls who had come knocking on his front door in an effort to save his soul. "This is even more of a reason for you to fuck off." Toby shook the dark memories from his mind and reached for a fresh spliff in the container behind the counter.

"I'm not a Jehovah's Witness," said the stranger in unison with the flint being sparked.

"Fine," Toby sighed as he got the joint burning, "good for you," he said between puffs "now for the last time," he exhaled a giant plume of indica, "we're closed and you need to get gone!"

"My journey has been a long one." The voice was calm and steady again. "It has involved many terrible ordeals." As before he grew ever more intense with each syllable until finally the stranger stopped speaking and rose up out of the beaten wooden chair like something from a horror movie. The figure stepped out from the cover of the shadows to reveal an averagely built man in his late fifties. Toby stared hard at him, figuring that all the drama was some kind of an indication that he should know this person, but for the life of him he couldn't think where on Earth he would know an old guy with a scruffy beard and an eye patch. Toby tried to recollect his days in prison where he had met a lot of odd characters and tussled with many of them. He stretched his mind back further to his days of dealing from the house, but nothing came to him. No memories of ever serving or slapping an old pirate rang a bell. Toby took another pull on the spliff and frowned at the stranger who stood staring at him from across the coffee shop. "It's not too surprising that you don't remember me," the man nodded his acknowledgement. "As I said, I have changed physically, mentally and spiritual—"

"This *is* a fucking God thing, innit?!" Toby cut him off and stood tall, facing the person now fucking his night up for him. He could feel the effects of all the other narcotics he'd consumed starting to wear off and wanted to slap the stranger for it. "I bloody knew it!" Toby took some big puffs on the spliff to try and stay calm, "All right, who or what are you then? Don't say Scientologist because that would be too much at this time of night, and let's face it that ain't even a real religion." Toby could feel the bile building up in his belly. "It's a cult!" He waved his arms frantically as he spat syllables at the stranger "Sure, the prick who started it is dead, but it's still a fucking cult in my opinion."

"This isn't a bloody religious thing you idiot!" the stranger barked at Toby and silenced him. "This is a fucking revenge thing!" He stepped closer and presented himself fully for Toby to see.

"Revenge?" Both the word and man were confusing Toby. Why would anyone seek revenge against him? He was just a cook. Sure, he was the best damn cook in the northern hemisphere, but that was no cause for revenge. If anything that would be envy.

"You slipped through my fingers in Belgium, where I almost

had you at that derelict farm," the man stepped closer as he spoke "Fucking minutes behind you I was!" He stepped closer again, and now Toby had a very tiny but real feeling way down in his gut that maybe, just maybe, this was someone from his past that he'd pissed off somehow. "You narrowly escaped my wrath in France multiple times due to outside intervention and the language barrier." The stranger gesticulated as his emotions started to rise yet again. "Your scent went cold on the water, and in England you had time on your side." The man was almost foaming at the mouth now. "But no more." He stared intensely at Toby, sure that there would finally be some recognition from his prey. "In Wales I was in a comma. Back home you had an advantage. But here and now—"

"What the fuck are you babbling about old man?" Toby was now figuring that he must be some nut job who'd taken too much acid and completely lost the plot. *Just my luck*, Toby thought, *after a nice quiet, easy and uneventful day, I've Jack Sparrow's deranged uncle to deal with.* "Who the fuck are you? What have you taken? And where can I get some?"

The stranger growled and stared maniacally at Toby as he proclaimed, "I am the Law!"

There were a few moments silence where Robert Thomas Law waited for Toby to finally remember him. Bob waited for the scruffy hippy he'd pursued multiple times and even arrested once to recall who he was.

"What?" the clueless stoner asked.

"Robert Thomas Law, former sergeant with the South Wales constabulary!"

"Who?"

"The fucking police officer who lost an eye, was put in a comma and left for dead after chasing you around Wales you stupid bastard!"

"Where?"

"The cop whose partner was shot dead by your boss!"

"Boss?"

"The man who is going to end your fucking life you no good hippie scumbag cunt!"

Bob was like a bear roaring at an intruder on his patch. Arms raised high, barely able to control his rage, feet stomping around the place.

"So this isn't a religious thing?" Toby now realised that he'd tuned out of the encounter at some point. Codeine had that effect on him, as it was meant to. Opioids would do that to you, cause you to drift in and out of conversations and indeed reality sometimes. Toby, who was keen on lacing his syrup with hallucinogens, was doubling down on his trips away from the real.

"You can pray to God to save your soul if you want boy, but your fucking arse is mine tonight." Bob pointed a steel-like finger at Toby, almost willing bullets to shoot out of it.

"Hey!" Toby was suddenly very alert again and back in the conversation. "This is a coffee shop, not a knocking shop," he pointed out, although it was not the same conversation Bob was having. "We're on the edge of the Red Light district here, not in it." Toby pointed out of the window at the barriers in the road. "If it's arse you want then you're in the wrong place. At the very least you'll have to wait until the animal comes back."

"You're fucking dead!" the man growled, fury writ large across his face.

"Shut up and get out of my coffee shop you cunt!" Toby could feel his old prison self-coming back to the surface. For a moment he could swear that he saw his two long-eared guides appear behind the Welsh pirate. There was now a very real concern inside of him that he was about to revisit his dark convict days. He knew he had to regain control of both his composure and the situation. Get the stranger, whoever he was, out of The Atom Café and then get very high and relaxed and forget about this nutter. That was the best course of action. The same one he did every night.

"Do you not understand what's going on here boy?" Bob was now unsure who was more confused, him or the hippie.

"I understand it's way past closing time and you shouldn't be here." Toby stepped forwards and pointed what remained of the spliff at what he now considered to be an intruder. "Now get out of my fucking coffee shop you Jack Sparrow wannabe!" Bob's patience immediately dissipated and he retrieved his revolver from within his thick and dirty coat. He cocked the hammer back and aimed it at his adversary all in one fluid motion. "Or stay and enjoy a nice cup of tea with a tasty muffin if you prefer." Toby felt his balls shrivel to the size of peanuts at the sight of the weapon. "They're blueberry," he smiled awkwardly. "Homemade." Toby stretched the awkward smile further across his narrow face and almost to breaking point before noticing that Bob's feet seemed to be adjusting to obtain better balance. *Better balance for what?* Toby pondered for the entire nanosecond it took him to realise that the cannon in Bob's hand probably had a hell of a kick to it and would require a sturdy hand to fire it accurately.

Toby belly-flopped his body onto the counter and scrambled to get over to the other side. It could hardly be called a leap and slide, more of a flop and fall. He crashed down to the other side with a thud and curse just as Bob started to unload the pistol in his hand. Each bullet from the revolver fired into the counter and wall beyond it, smashing glass and mirror, sending fragments and splinters of the wooden counter into the air and filling the coffee shop with thunderous explosions and the pungent smell of the nitro-glycerine propellant.

"Two fucking years ago a fellow brother in blue was killed because of you!" Bob bellowed as he reloaded the pistol's chamber and started walking toward the counter. Images of his dead partner Dave flashed through his mind's eye and reminded him of that fateful day when his path crossed Toby's and forever changed him for the worse. "I'm going to make you pay boy! You'll pay in screams and blood! You'll pay for making me chase you all over Wales! You'll pay for making me chase you to fuckin' Amsterdam!" Bob reached the counter and caught his reflection in what was left of the shattered mirror behind it. "You'll pay for my fucking eye!" Bob stalked the length of the counter until he reached the entrance to walk behind it. He leaped quickly and aimed his pistol to where Toby had landed "You'll pay for the murder of my fucking partner you—" the lack of an enemy to shoot where there should be one caused Bob to stop ranting. He stared confused at the small space behind the counter, which had nowhere to hide that he couldn't see from where he was stood.

As the stranger ranted and fired shots into Toby's beloved coffee shop he decided that it was time to initiate his 'Plan B'. The plan had been mocked and considered a waste of time when he first talked about it, but now here he was in the exact situation he had predicted would happen and ready to go through with it.

Toby lifted the hatch to the cellar, which was almost invisible to someone who didn't already know it was there, and carefully slid down to the ladder, closing the hatch silently behind him. The six booms from the gun meant that there was little chance the intruder would hear what was happening, but Toby needed to ensure he had sufficient time to carry the plan out and stock up on supplies.

'Supplies' consisted of drugs and drug paraphernalia. He casually perused the shelves that lined both sides of the concrete tunnel, all overflowing with stock for the coffee shop, his illegal business and personal consumption. Technically all three of these constituted the same thing to Toby. He shrugged his thick coat on and then promptly began stuffing all of his pockets with Ziploc bags of weed, vacuum-sealed magic mushrooms, rolling papers, blocks of hashish, bottles of syrup, lighters, fat wraps of cocaine and a small Tupperware box full of crystal meth. Once he thought he was sufficiently stocked, or at least there was no more room left in his pockets, he lit a spliff and listened for any signs of the intruder finding the hatch down into the basement. The only sounds were the footfalls of the pirate guy on broken glass pacing up and down the length of the counter. Before he turned to leave he remembered that there were some sheets of acid in an envelope that may come in handy. Toby hurried into the lab, slid a few of the flat sheets into what little space remained in a pocket and then walked to the end of the tunnel where a heavy metal door was set into the concrete wall. Before exiting through the door Toby pulled a red handle down attached to a pipe that ran the length of the tunnel, dropped the half-smoked spliff onto the bare concrete floor and then closed the large exit behind him with a thud. He tried not to dwell on his actions, they were after all a vital necessity to his survival. The madman in the coffee shop was clearly out to kill Toby, and therefore drastic and extreme action needed to be taken.

Toby snatched up the torch he'd left on the other side of the door for his 'Plan B' and then swiftly made his way along the passageway that had sharp corners taking him away from the coffee shop and under De Wallen. The concrete floor reflected his torch light due to all of the water that passed down there from the canals. Toby knew that a heavy fall of rain could cause these tunnels to fill with water making them unusable, but he had to take a chance when designing his escape route and the discovery of this medieval network of tunnels originally intended for prevention of the canals over flowing above him was too good an opportunity to be overlooked. Sure, they were dangerous and off-limits for much of autumn and yes they stank like Satan's sphincter, but all in all it was a genius exit strategy unknown to anyone other than him and his partner.

Toby suddenly realised that he should find Mark and inform him of the implementation of 'Plan B'. There was a very high probability that his friend would figure it out for himself, but there was no guarantee he was within earshot.

The cramped and almost pitch-black corridor made passing each other difficult, but the women were used to it as they had all been working the windows for many months now, some even for years. Nobody complained about it, you just accepted that these were the working conditions. The girls ensured not to hang around in the space as that made life difficult for the others to get back and forth between bedrooms and the bathrooms. Occasionally customers had to walk the corridor too if the girls felt they needed a wash or they'd had too much to drink.

Toby entered from a secret door in the wall that slid open, even moving the neon tubes near the ceiling. It was master craftsmanship made all the more concealed by the poor lighting. None of the prostitutes were particularly shocked or surprised when the wall suddenly shook and slid sideways, releasing a thick plume of pungent skunk smoke. Toby had practiced the escape multiple times when he originally discovered it and had warned the women that one day he may emerge from it without warning. What he didn't know was that his friend and partner-in-crime had been regularly using it as an easier way to get from The Atom Café to the red-lit windows to have his wicked way with the women of the night on many an occasion.

The girls smiled at Toby as he closed the secret passageway behind him and then walked past the cubicles along the corridor until one of the bikini-clad vixens raised an eyebrow and pointed a long shiny fingernail at a closed door. Toby nodded and smiled his appreciation for the information before barging straight into the room emitting loud rock music.

Toby strode forwards and immediately started yelling over the music, "It's happened dude! Plan B—" but he couldn't finish the sentence or his chain of thought. In all the years he and Mark had been friends and partners they had done a lot of fucked-up things together. Toby had witnessed Mark partake in any number of sexual misadventures. Never though, with or without Mark, had Toby seen what his drug-glazed eyes now saw before him.

In the standard window room, behind closed red curtains and illuminated by light-pink neon strips, surrounded by the bare plastic and wood furnishings, stood an eight foot wooden X.

Strapped to the cross with leather belts and chrome chains was his oldest friend, Mark Anthony King. As always, Mark still wore his gold-rimmed Elvis Presley sunglasses, despite being in near complete blackness, and one other item. In his stretched mouth was a giant red ball gag, which caused Mark to drool uncontrollably over the back of the cross that his bare chest and stomach pressed up against. Toby slowly circled around his friend spread eagled to the large wooden apparatus, taking in the sight of his naked and oiled body that bore multiple red lines across its flesh. The bite of the whip for the most part looked fresh. Mark's skin glinted under the neon tubes due to the obscene amount of oil he was covered in. Toby was shocked and concerned at the sight, as Mark's torso was against the wood, which meant the only sexual acts he could partake in involved him receiving and not giving. It was at that point Toby stopped circling his naked friend and turned to face the other two occupants of the room.

"Hey Tess," he said to the blonde in her mid-twenties. "Lola," he nodded to the busty dominatrix with long black hair.

"Hi Toby," Tess replied with a little wave and cheeky smile, completely unfazed by his sudden intrusion on the scene.

"Just in time," Lola added with a few sharp thrusts of her hips.

"For what?" Toby naively enquired as he looked down at her thrusting hips to see the giant plastic strap-on cock that she was wearing. He jumped back in shock at both the unexpected sight and the size of the thing. Toby also observed at this point what Tess was doing. In her hand was the bottle of oil, or lubricant of some kind at least, that Mark was covered in. Only now she was lathering it all over the strap on. The horror of the scene suddenly dawned on Toby as he realised that this was the reason Mark was strapped to the giant X-frame stomach first. This was why he drooled over the ball gag.

"Oh, come on honey," Lola purred through large pouty lips "Don't tell auntie Lola that you've never been pegged before." Now she rocked her hips more gently, as if hinting to Toby that she would take it easier on his rectum than Mark's should he care to partake.

"Never!" Toby screamed quickly, taking another step back in fright.

"Would you like to be?" Tess enquired seductively "We have another one," she said as she rubbed the giant piece of solid plastic in the most erotic of ways. It turned Toby on to see this, but also frightened him to think about what she was asking him. He shook his head back into reality and backed away from perverted day dreams of him and Tess, but without the plastic just the oil. He walked around the X, away from the pros, to look Mark in the face. It took Toby a moment to compose himself and get past the sight of Mark's lips squeezing down on the large red orb rammed into his mouth. The dribble cascading down onto the back of the X was leaving glistening streaks in its wake – the whole sordid scene in general left him feeling unnerved. Toby knew Mark was an animal, but he didn't realise that his sexual misadventures had sunk to the level of being fucked in the arse with a giant strap-on worn by a dominatrix. Sure, Lola was a scorching hot piece of arse in Toby's opinion and well worth taking the time out of your day to have fun with. But she was a hard-core dominatrix and insisted that pleasure always be accompanied by pain to truly appreciate the act of sex.

"We need to talk dude," Toby informed his partner.

"I'm kinda busy," Mark said. Or at least that's what Toby thought he said through muffled and obstructed mouth movements. The conversation continued, but most of it had to be interpreted by Toby rather than heard.

"This," Toby pointed at the sight before him, "can wait."

"Hell no!" Mark mumbled, causing more of a saliva waterfall. "They charge for every 20 minutes." Mark's eyebrows raised to indicate the seriousness of the situation and financial burden Toby was placing on him.

"We need to leave," Toby instructed his partner, "now!" He then started trying to figure out how to undo Mark and get him off the frame.

"We're just getting started," Mark protested.

Toby stopped his attempt at freeing Mark from his bonds, suddenly realising that he may not react well to the next bit of news that he needed to be given and that his being restrained could save Toby from a slap or 10. "The coffee shop is…" Toby rocked his head from side-to-side trying to find the appropriate word, "…gone."

"*Gone?*" Mark sprayed.

Toby nodded confirmation that he had heard him correctly over the music and then followed that up with his best *I'm innocent* smile, which of course just made him look all the more guilty.

"How the fuck can it be fucking gone?" Mark drooled furiously after Toby partially loosened the ball gag.

"Somebody found me," Toby thought that sounded too much like it was his fault. "It," he followed up, to imply 'they' found the café not him and therefor it wasn't his fault. "Us," he then thought it best to include Mark in any accusations of guilt or wrongdoing.

"But how can an entire fucking coffee shop be gone?" Mark leaked the question over the X, unsure whether he actually wanted to know the answer or not.

"I think he said he was a cop…" Toby wondered out loud. He wasn't 100% sure of the accuracy of this information or if he had already mentioned it to Mark. There were still a lot of drugs in his system and the peculiarity of the surroundings he currently found himself in were slightly unhinging him. "He was wearing an eye patch," Toby recalled. "Like a fucking pirate," he added this like it implied he was innocent of anything else that had occurred.

"Explain *gone* Toby!" Mark drooled, fearful that he already knew the answer.

"Then he said something about being chased and someone died," Toby tried to recount what Bob had been saying before shooting at him. "Yeah, there was definitely a murder involved somewhere in his story."

"What did you do?!" Mark screeched from behind the gag. He'd heard more than enough of his partner's drug-fuelled ramblings. He'd wasted more than enough of the time he should have spent having debauched fuck-fun with Tess and Lola rather than listening to Toby babble. Mark knew that his friend had concocted a very crazy and unfortunately very real escape plan that he swore would only ever be used in the most extreme of circumstances, and now feared it had been implemented tonight.

"...but with our past that could mean anything anywhere," Toby continued to ramble out loud. "Between all that shit that went down back at the house and then my time behind bars—"

"The coffee shop Toby!" Mark screamed this so loud he almost opened his mouth wide enough to say it clearly past the ball gag. "Tell me what fucking happened to The Atom Café!" Mark needed to hear it from Toby. Had he just fucked him up the arse metaphorically instead of letting Lola do it literally? Mark would have preferred the Lola option, but the look in his partner's eyes coupled with his rambling had now convinced Mark that Toby's ludicrous Plan B had been enacted.

"He may have mentioned the French Connection too," Toby continued to blabber. "I can't quite recall, but I know he was Welsh." Toby was actually lost in the conversation now. "He called me a hippie for sure," Toby nodded at what he was sure was an accurate memory of the night's earlier events. "Did I mention he only had one eye?" Toby perked up as he asked this, thinking that it was an integral part of the story. "I'm not sure about the leg, it may have been wooden but I can't be—"

"Shut up about the fucking pirate Toby!"

"He shot at me dude! Several times!" Toby couldn't understand why Mark had such little interest in the other key player of the story. "With a hand cannon!" It must be because he didn't fully appreciate the severity of the story. "A great big fuck off machine gun!" Toby wasn't sure if he had embellished that last part, but it certainly sounded good.

"What happened to the goddamn coffee shop Toby?!" Mark tried to break out of his restraints with frustration and fear that Toby had done what he thought he had.

"Okay, fine!" Toby decided that it was time to give Mark that last detail of the story. "I did Plan B. I had to."

"YOU DID WHAT?!" Mark shook the X frantically. He had already figured that Toby had done it, but upon hearing the confession he freaked out and wanted to wrap his hands around his business partner's scrawny neck. He wanted to remind him of the large pile of shit that he had just landed them in. He had always worried that Toby would one day do it accidentally, a result of another one of his daily drug binges, and now that he'd heard his ramblings of pirates and police and machine guns he was sure that Toby had done too much meth and then implemented the plan prematurely.

"I told you! I had to!" Toby yelled at his partner's sunglasses that reflected his own stupidity right back at him. "It was all part of my big escape plan in case of an emergency like the one I had tonight," Toby realised how much his last statement incriminated him, and him alone. *"Our plan B."* He tried to drag Mark in on the accountability for what he'd done.

"Couldn't you have just run away?"

"He had a big fucking gun!"

"You're a cunt!"

Toby was visibly offended, but tried to play it off. "What?" He looked away from his partner, "I can't understand you with the…" Toby waved at his own mouth to indicate the ball gag in Mark's, now openly showing that he was shocked by the whole sordid scene around him again.

"CUNT! C-U-mother-fucking-N-T! You are a useless cunt!" Mark moved his head side to side with each syllable, occasionally snapping his neck forwards to spray spit at his partner.

"Still not getting it."

"Time's up sweetie," Lola suddenly interrupted the conversation.

Mark's face turned red enough to heat the whole city as he shook with rage and almost shat all over the floor while staring daggers at his partner and screeching once again through the ball gag, "CU—"

And then the whole room and building it occupied shook from the giant explosion that was Plan B and the destruction of The Atom Café that could be heard even from this distance and above the loud music blasting in the small confines. Toby knew he'd heard the last from Pirate Bob, whoever that nutter was.

"—NT!" Mark finished his expletive and knew that their idyllic lives in Amsterdam had just come to an end.

Chapter 2 – Past

Toby's Time in Prison

Toby paced back and forth like a caged lion. The prison cell was small, but his short strides made it seem like he was walking in a far larger enclosure. His manic steps made him look crazier than his outward appearance already did. His hair was unkempt and stubble getting thicker. He'd been in prison for several months now and the lack of decent hard drugs combined with all of the obscene violence had made for quite an unhinged degenerate.

His unravelling mind flittered between memories of the day everything went horribly wrong and the dozen people who lost their lives, the day the judge had sentenced him to life in prison and the numerous violent clashes he'd had with both guards and inmates behind the walls where he now lived. He needed drugs, he knew that for sure. He couldn't simply go cold turkey and hope to survive intact – not mentally intact anyway. Any plans for getting clean needed to be done under strict conditions that involved a gradual reduction in his dosage. The shit being sold in the prison wasn't good enough to either keep him high or help him come down at a safe and regulated pace. Toby knew that he needed to get back to doing what he did best and dose himself appropriately.

He was almost as unaware of their presence in the room as he was of his own incoherent muttering and frantic pacing. He'd been rambling gibberish to himself under his breath for almost an hour now as he paced up and down the grey cell while alternating between gnawing at his nails and making wild and violent hand gestures that communicated nothing in particular other than he really was losing it. In the doorway they stood and watched, unsure of how long they should wait and observe before either making some kind of sound to alert Toby of their arrival or just turn and leave so that they wouldn't have to deal with the madman who had acquired quite the reputation in a short amount of time.

Harrison and Niall had served a lot of time in various prisons both in the UK and abroad. They were hardcore criminals, career outlaws, but they had never served time with someone like Toby. As far as they were concerned he shouldn't even be in a real prison, he should be in a mental institution with the rest of the crazies. Now, standing in his secure unit and observing him almost as you would an animal in a zoo, they questioned if they were doing the right thing by agreeing to meet him in his cell hidden from the rest of the prison, their gang and the guards. Sure, they were both giants compared to Toby. They were both avid bodybuilders and juicers. They were both tooled up with rudimentary but effective shanks and had their hands inside their hoodie pockets tightly gripping their weapons of choice. But Toby was a lunatic who had been sentenced to life for murder and cannibalism. Toby was the nutter who regularly bit people's faces off when they fucked with him. Toby was basically crazy and highly unpredictable as far as they were concerned.

"Drugs!" Toby suddenly yelled upon realising that Harrison and Niall were stood inside his cell. Both of the bodybuilders flinched at the sudden bark, but forced themselves to appear icy cool and collected on the surface. "Good drugs," Toby continued while he stood facing the men from the other side of the cell, both surprising and confusing the two of them who watched closely for any signs of violence that may suddenly erupt. "The fucking best drugs!"

There was a moment of awkward, uneasy silence before Harrison finally asked, "What?"

"Fucking drugs man!" Toby squealed in response to what in his mind was a stupid question.

"What about drugs you—" Niall stopped himself short of insulting Toby. Sure, he was one of the toughest men to be born in Ireland. Sure, he was a member of a violent and murderous biker gang that held a lot of power behind the prison walls. And sure, Niall had been in countless fights and beaten dozens of men to a bloody pulp. But he had seen the results of what happened to other prisoners who had messed with Toby and he was in no rush to try his chances. If it came to a fight, then he'd stand his ground no problem but there was no need to push things in that direction needlessly.

"Are you looking to cop mate?" Harrison finally broke the uneasy silence that had filled the air when Niall had stopped himself from provoking Toby.

"Cop? COP?! Fucking cop he says like the fucking nee-na-nee-na..." Toby started pacing again to the sounds of his imitation of a police siren. His eyes grew wide with delirium and the two bikers who watched him grew ever more uneasy with the situation they found themselves in. Despite being stood directly in front of the unlocked and slightly ajar cell door, they both felt trapped in the six by eight box with the foaming cannibal.

"If it's drugs you're after, we can hook you up no problem fella," Harrison spoke confidently and reassuringly. "Just tell us what you're after." He figured that all of the rumours about this prisoner must be true, the aftermath of his vicious battles along with the weirdness they were watching now was all the proof he needed.

"As long as you've got the funds," Niall added in a less friendly tone.

Toby was suddenly right there in the Irish man's face. Harrison felt like it had taken less time than it took to blink and suddenly the lunatic was in his brother-in-arms' personal space with a look of hunger spread over his cannibal chops. Harrison and Niall had been riding hogs and living the outlaw life together for many years now, and despite Harrison being English and Niall being Irish there had never been any quarrels, differences or arguments between them. Now, however, Harrison felt like his Celtic comrade was being a little foolish pushing the other prisoner's buttons.

"Fuck fucking funds man!" Toby yelled into the Irish man's square jaw that lined up with Toby's eyes. "Fuck fucking copping!" he squealed as he sprang to his right and into the face of the English man. "I'm the fucking cook! Not just *A* cook, *THE* fucking cook!" Toby stepped back, nodding confirmation to the two bikers with a maniac stare and wild hand gestures. "I'm a fucking legend in my own lifetime man. A master craftsman. A god among the gifted. A fucking, fucking, master fucking chemist, fucking genius like fucking you know, fucking—"

"You mean, you're on drugs?" Harrison asked cautiously. He was unsure if this is what the madman was trying to tell them or if the suggestion would insult him, but he was both confused and losing his patience now. Harrison turned to Niall for confirmation that the crazy must be high on something. Niall nodded his silent agreement before looking back at the pacing prisoner.

"They're not listening to you," Toby said to himself. "They're not understanding you Toby. They're fucking amateurs dude. They don't realise what a turn this is for them, they're fucking clueless." Toby stopped ranting to laugh maniacally to himself.

Behind the howling Toby, Harrison looked at his partner and then nodded at the door as a sign to exit. Niall again nodded confirmation that he was in agreement with the English man. But before they could make their escape Toby was bounding back across the room and into their faces, screaming, "Go? GO! You can't go." He side-stepped and lunged between the two men who were each twice his size while continuously ranting, "Going nowhere, going to say yes, going to do business, fucking TCB boys, drugs, drug business – my business. Me. You. Cook. Sell. Fucking drugs, man." Toby stopped his tirade momentarily in order to nod emphatically, like an epileptic trying to use a jackhammer. "Well?! Are you in boys?"

The two bikers looked at each other for an explanation, but each was as clueless as the other. They turned their attention back to Toby.

"In what?" Harrison enquired.

The question was answered by a high-pitched sound like you would expect a pig to make if it were sodomised by an elephant on industrial-strength Viagra. The sound pushed the bikers past uneasy to frightened and both revealed the weapons they had brought to the meeting. Niall gripped the shank in his right hand and had his giant left hand balled into a fist ready to destroy Toby's jaw like it was made of matchsticks. Harrison's weapon of choice were his fists, but adorned with very worn and battered brass knuckle dusters. The sight of the weapons caused Toby to stop rambling and take a step back while inhaling and exhaling sharply.

"Okay, okay," Toby said calmly as he backed away. "I realise my sales pitches can be a little... unorthodox at times, but that's why I should just be cooking not selling. Manufacturing not marketing, that's the key thing to remember when dealing..." Toby trailed off at the realisation that the two men before him were very confused. What he didn't realise is that they weren't so much confused about his proposal, but whether or not they should attack him, keep listening or simply walk away. Toby took several deep breaths and tried to pep talk himself mentally into just being as normal as possible for a couple of minutes. Just long enough to explain his proposal to the representatives of one of the most feared biker gangs in all of Europe. "I am offering to cook drugs for you. Here in prison," he began calmly enough. "I cook," he repeated, and closed his eyes to concentrate very hard on not slipping back into high-pitched squeals and ranting. "You sell," he opened his eyes and felt his eyebrows stretch up his head with the strain of talking like a normal human being. "Bring me the ingredients and I'll make the best shit you've ever smoked, swallowed or stuck a vein with." Toby breathed deep as he smiled wide and spread his arms like some world-famous sports star who had just scored the winning point to finish the championship.

Harrison lowered his metal knuckles before asking, "Cook what, exactly?"

"Anything," Toby answered matter-of-factly. "Everything," he said with a look of confusion, not understanding why the 'roid-heads were unable to grasp the simple premise that they were dealing with a narcotic Gordon Ramsay. "I'll cook shit that doesn't have a name yet, but it'll have every swinging dick in this place begging for more." He spelled it out for them as simply as he could manage. He kind of reminded himself of Mark, his dead friend and business partner.

"And what do you want?" Niall asked, still confused.

"To cook. It's what I do. It's who I am."

"That's it?" Harrison couldn't believe his ears.

Toby looked down at the stained concrete beneath his feet and suddenly became very coy and sheepish. "Well, I may want to do a little myself too." Toby was suddenly aware that they may not understand he was still a master even when indulging in his own wares. "Strictly in a professional capacity of course." He tried to sell it like a positive thing, which of course it was in his eyes. "Quality control and the like – I'm sure you understand." Toby nodded and looked very serious. "A man with my reputation has standards that must be maintained."

"We already have our own shit to sell," Harrison said bluntly. The Grim Union were a long-established gang who had members locked up in prisons all over Europe and elsewhere in the world. In every prison they got banged up in they made themselves known and started some kind of business involving the selling of narcotics as well as other things. In the UK the bikers had been in and out of the prison system for many years and had contacts and connections everywhere. They had no need of an in-house cook due to their fellow bikers on the outside smuggling the gear in for them, as well as some of the guards who took bribes or could be coerced into doing what the gang wanted.

"That's why I came to you guys," Toby stated like it was the most obvious thing in the world. "Fucking genius like, innit?" As far as he was concerned, it only made sense to cook for the guys doing the most sales. He intended to produce vast quantities of drugs and would require a large sales network to accommodate his supply, regardless of the demand his gear would undoubtedly create over any existing drug problems within the penitentiary. The looks on the biker's faces told Toby they didn't fully comprehend and would require further explanation.

"I see what goes down in this place," Toby began another rant. "You and your apes smuggle shit in to sell all the time, so sure I could've gone to the man, the fucking man with a plan, struck a deal with the guards to bring me the shit to cook and then have them knock it out. But they're the fucking man, man. The man's the fucking reason I'm rotting behind bars instead of cooking up a storm in another kitchen of my own desire. The man put me in this shit – he thinks I don't fucking know, but I know, I fucking know man. So, fuck the guards! Fuck the man! And fuck his plan! I'm following my own plan man, and it's a great fucking plan if you just shut the fuck up and fucking listen for a second, will You? Huh? For me, could you just fucking, for me, just fucking listen for one tiny, little… Drugs! Are we in business?! Course we're in business. You ain't fucking stupid, not even for gorilla bikers. So, it's agreed. I'll give you boys a list, a recipe, a fucking you-know-what of the you-know-who, and then we can get fucking to it. Me, you and the whole fucking jungle. It'll be glorious, boys, fucking fan-dabby-dozy-tastic with a feather in its cap and a—" Toby suddenly stopped his mad rambling, a look of urgency on his face and said, "Speaking of feathers, you boys aren't allergic are you?"

The two burly bikers sporting tattoos and shaved heads were momentarily too stunned to speak. When they did manage to focus again they had to look at each other for guidance, of which none could be given by either.

"What?" Harrison finally asked.

"Are we allergic to feathers?" Niall asked the question for confirmation, but felt very foolish doing so. It seemed the most bizarre query to be asking at that moment in time.

"Allergic to…?" Toby almost lost his shit at their inability to follow his train of thought. "Feathers…?" He trembled with rage and almost pulled his own hair out. "What the fuck are you babbling about man? There's no feathers in crank or any of the other shit I'm gonna cook up." Toby couldn't believe that they couldn't follow his very simple chain of thought.

"You can cook crank?" asked a suddenly very interested Niall.

"In here?" followed up Harrison, equally as intrigued.

"Have you not been fucking listening? Have you not followed a single fucking word that I've been saying?" Toby forced himself to suppress the desire to insult the gangsters before him. "*YES!* I can cook crank and a bunch of other shit, better shit, right here in this shithole! You just need to get me the cooking utensils and the ingredients, 'cos old Toby already has the recipe right up here." He ended his words with several violent jabs to the temple with an index finger while smiling and nodding like someone already very high on meth. After a lot of masochistic head prodding he stopped attacking himself and ceased smiling before stating matter-of-factly, "Right then. Fine. Good boys.

You drive a hard bargain, the pair of you, but it's a deal. I'm in." The madman then dropped down onto his thin and dirty mattress sat atop the creaky cot. Toby then proceeded to retrieve a novel from beneath his pillow and continued reading it from where he had left off, like Harrison and Niall were no longer even in the room with him. They stood staring at him, dumbfounded. After it became painfully clear that Toby was no longer participating in a conversation or the meeting due to the importance of the book in his hand, the bikers nodded at one another that it was finally time to leave the cell.

The bodybuilder bikers put their hands and weapons back into the pockets of their hoodies and calmly, silently, strolled out of Toby's cell and along the tier that it was situated on and overlooked the ground floor. Once he was sure that he was out of earshot, Niall asked, "What the fuck just happened?"

"I think we just got ourselves an in-house cook," Harrison replied, although not fully confident with his own answer. "*Maybe*."

"But he's fucking crazy!"

"One of the screws told me he was a cook on the outside."

"So?" Niall didn't care if he really could cook crank, he was still a dangerous lunatic. "Why the fuck do you want him to cook for us?"

"He was some kind of whiz kid. Top of his class at university and all that."

"That mad bastard?!"

"A mad professor," Harrison retorted. "Anyway, we'll give him a try." As far as Harrison was concerned, he was the ranking club member in this prison and had final say on all decisions. "If he cooks good and we make coin, great." The others never disagreed with him anyway. His smarts are what got him in the position of power he was in. "If he fucks up, we kill him." As powerful as he was in the prison it was his ruthlessness that kept him there on top. "Simple."

Niall nodded his agreement.

"Get word out to the brothers. We're going to need some supplies."

The first tier was one of the coldest and most depressing in the entire prison. It looked Third World and like you could catch any number of diseases just by stepping foot on it, yet alone from all the vicious rapes that occurred in there. When Toby had first arrived at the prison the shower block had been the place that frightened him the most. For years he'd been watching movies and TV dramas that depicted giant muscular prison predators raping skinny white fish in the slippery confines of the prison showers. He could just picture Mark laughing and making jokes about not attempting to pick up any dropped bars of soap if he were still alive to come and visit or receive calls. That first shower he had taken he'd done so fully clothed, with his boots on and back to the wall, clutching the only weapons he'd managed to acquire: a plastic spoon from the canteen and his toothbrush. If anyone made eye contact with him he had whimpered and looked down at the wet, germ-infested concrete.

Now it was very different. Today he stood bollock naked with no weapons and stared hard at all present. These days it was the other prisoners who avoided making eye contact with the cannibal whose reputation preceded him. At first, the reputation was just exaggerated but now it was technically true. Everyone knew that he hadn't only been hit with drug arraignments, but also multiple murder and cannibalism charges. What they didn't know is that Toby was innocent of most of the murders and all of the cannibalism. However, since being incarcerated that had technically changed due to the ferocity of his fights. There were many a prisoner and guard missing an ear or their nose, a finger or even just chunks of their face, throat or body because they had provoked Toby, who had in return responded in the most violent and psychotic way imaginable. This is why he stood under the ice-cold water and stared out at the wash room and the several naked men who hurriedly hosed themselves down before quickly departing from his demented gaze.

After all of the other prisoners had finished their ultra-fast showers and slip-slided all the way out to a safer environment, Toby continued to stand and stare at nothing. When the prison guard entered to check that everyone had finished he paid little attention to the lunatic staring off into the middle distance, he just noticed there was one prisoner still left in there.

"Let's finish up," the guard said casually, "shower time's over."

Toby continued to stare from under the cascading water that most prisoners felt was too cold to stand in for any length of time. He looked like some kind of East Asian martial arts master stood beneath a waterfall to enhance their zen while meditating. Only he had bad posture and a Private Pile glare to him.

"Toby, let's not fuck around today, yeah?" the guard said once he noticed not only who he was dealing with but also the crazy look in the convict's eyes. "Right now. I'm not in the mood." The guard attempted to sound as authoritative as possible. He was only slightly taller than Toby, but nowhere near as skinny. He was sure he could take him in a fight if it came to it. The prisoner was naked, wet and unarmed. "Dry off and get back to your cell."

"You're crooked, right?" Toby leaned slightly forwards out of the falling water to ask the guard who was visibly insulted.

"What'd I just say to you?"

"I'm not fucking around," Toby answered the rhetorical question. "I'm serious," he said with a nod. "You're crooked," he continued to nod as he spoke. "And I want to make a deal."

The guard checked his surroundings. Firstly, to ensure he hadn't just walked into some kind of trap. He was sure this wasn't the case as Toby wasn't affiliated with anyone, but he had to be sure. Also, to check there was nobody listening to the conversation that was about to be had. "What you after?"

"I'm going to start cooking again," Toby informed the guard. "I need the screws to stay out of my shit."

"Ever heard of discretion?" the guard asked.

"Fuck discreet. I'm going to be doing major shit here soon. Big cooks, vast quantities of crazy fucking cocktails. I'll be doing too much to stay hidden. Sure, I could cook smaller batches. Different drugs. But, I'm the cook. I cook what I like. It'll be big. It'll stink this fucking joint out no end. I can't be having your lot interrupting me when I'm balls-deep in it." Toby grabbed his scrotum upon spitting the word 'balls' at the guard for emphasis.

The guard checked for unwelcome ears once more before asking, "So, what do you think I can do for your enterprise?"

"Make sure the screws know it's in their best interest to stay away," Toby made flapping motions with his hands like he was shooing away an insulant child. "Turn a blind eye," he damn near poked both index fingers into his sockets. "Pretend they can't smell nothing," he sniffed the air emphatically and loudly. "Make like they don't hear nothing," he placed his index fingers into his ears for a few moments before whispering, "Act like I'm a ghost, yeah?"

The guard knew that dealing with the madman could be dangerous, but he also knew that there was a lot of money to be made when it came to shifting drugs, and even more when it came to drugs and prisoners. He and several of the other guards had been smuggling and selling drugs for many years. Usually prisoners who attempted to make drugs inside either produced shit that nobody wanted or got aggressively shut down by the warden and guards. Still, money is a harsh mistress to turn your back on.

"Let's say I get the others on board," the guard folded his arms across his chest and spoke in a tone that ensured Toby understood he was interested, but still far from decided as there was a crucial element that had not been addressed yet. "What's in it for me?"

"The shit I'll be cooking will be so good you can flog it on the outside."

"Bollocks!" The guard roared with laughter. He'd heard it all now. Even with the right connections and master smugglers, getting the quality supplies to make high-grade narcotics was impossible inside a prison. And now the lunatic was claiming to be able to make gear good enough to smuggle out of the prison to sell on the streets where everything and anything was already available. Ridiculous!

Between bursts of laughter the guard noticed that Toby had stepped out from under the icy water and was striding in his direction, shrivelled shlong leading the way. The guard tightened his grip on the baton in his hand and readied it to swing at the side of the prisoner's head should he try to use his minuscule member on him or attack in any other way.

"The only bollocks here are these hairy fuckers," Toby grabbed his shrunken scrotum covered in matted curls. "My shit's the shit!" he barked into the guards slightly elevated face. "And that ain't no shit."

"This is a prison Toby," the guard said calmly. He was sure this could all be resolved with logic, despite dealing with a cannibal. "Sure, you can cook stuff – that's nothing new. But the gear prisoners cook on the inside can't ever come close to what people are knocking up on the outside. You just don't have the supplies or the resourc—"

"I do," Toby cut him off, realising he wasn't yet aware of all the facts to be making informed statements.

"What?"

"I struck a deal with the Union," Toby informed him with a wide-eyed nod.

"The Grim Union?" the guard asked tentatively, knowing that even mentioning their name in the wrong context could lead to trouble further on down the line.

"No, the fucking workers' union. Of course the Grim," Toby stated the obvious. "They bring me the shit, I cook it, they flog it. Simple."

"They'll fucking kill you for telling me this," the guard said shaking his head in disbelief. The age-old saying behind bars was 'snitches get stitches', but as far as the Grim Union bikers were concerned snitches got gang raped to death. They may even kill the guard for just knowing this information.

"No, they won't," Toby informed him like it was a straight-up fact. "Once I start cooking, you – them – everyone will see that I'm the fucking *cook*," he spread his arms majestically. "And everyone will want the same thing." Toby stepped back and nodded.

"And what's that?"

"*More*," he said with further frantic nodding of his head.

Toby bounced around his cell like a small child at Christmas, only not so innocent-looking. He went from item to item, expecting it and trying his best to ensure not only it was what he needed but that it was in decent working order. He knew that for some of the equipment it would be impossible to tell if it was functioning properly until he had it hooked up and got it running, but the more items he checked the more he realised there was less chance of a fuck-up occurring later.

A chain gang of four Grim Union bikers made a line from the far wall to the landing outside his cell door from where they shifted the various boxes. There were some big and heavy pieces of equipment that Toby knew he would struggle with, but the tattooed bodybuilders made it look easy. Harrison and Niall appeared almost identical to their Dutch comrade Lars. All three looked like they could be poster boys for some Nazi men's health magazine, with their shaved heads and bulging veins running over swollen muscles wreathed in tattoos that were mostly images of death, sex and horror. The fourth biker, Yago, only differed in that he had dark brown skin due to him being a Spaniard.

The Grim Union were a rarity in the penal system. A mixed-race gang from multiple countries. They were originally formed in Lars' homeland, but had spread out all over Europe and had been particularly popular in the UK. Now, they had infiltrated almost every major city, port and prison throughout the continent and used whatever means they could in order to make illegal cash quickly. Being a biker gang meant that moving around was simply a part of their lifestyle and not the inconvenience many organised criminals considered it to be. This also enabled their swift expansion over the mainland. The ease of which they rode from city to city, starting shit with the local criminal gangs and then either obliterating them or taking them into the horde allowed them to expand everywhere at speed. The name said it all: it had been chosen that way most people figured. The Grim Union, meaning that most who joined did so under threat of something grim happening to them if they didn't. Of course, once you were part of the pack there are many advantages to be had.

"Are you fucking sure about this?" Harrison asked Toby one more time. He still couldn't wrap his head around the idea that the guards wouldn't just smash up all of the equipment the moment they saw it. Even under the protection of the bikers, there were some liberties that the guards couldn't be seen to overlook and building an entire chemical cookhouse in your cell blatantly crossed that line between acceptable and downright piss-take.

"Yes," Toby simply replied while continuing to check his new toys.

"And why the guards won't stop you?" Lars asked.

"I made a deal," Toby answered without really thinking about the fact he was treading on a lot of thin ice with that statement.

"You did what?!" barked Harrison.

"You said you didn't want to deal with the fucking screws!" Niall bellowed.

"Like he said," Toby stopped and turned to face Harrison and Niall while pointing at the Dutchman, "why wouldn't they just stop me and take everything?" He paused, but knew nobody would attempt to answer the rhetorical question. "Because I give them a little something. They turn a blind eye, I cook, you sell, the cons all get high and the guards get some to flog on the outside." Toby cocked his head to one side, "Everyone's a fucking winner."

"You should have spoken to us about this first," Harrison rumbled through gritted teeth that almost shattered the vice-like pressure of his clenched jaw.

"Why?" Toby couldn't understand what difference it would have made considering it was an essential step to accomplish his goal. "It doesn't concern you."

"Doesn't—?" Harrison's jaw prevented him from ending his sentence. The muscles tightened up to where they almost contracted in on themselves like an imploding super nova. The colour of his skin that struggled to stay on his skull from being pulled so tight also mirrored that of an impending nuclear meltdown. After a few moments of violent vibrating in his big black Jack boots he managed to state, "We're in this together Toby." Harrison's fists almost popped they were clenched so tightly at his sides. The pupils of his eyes seemed to stretch out across the prison cell to shank the chemist.

"Sure we are," Toby said nonchalantly, like a disinterested lover to a soon-to-be ex. "But I'm the cook and I'll get this shit done." Toby turned back to his new equipment while assuring the biker, "I'm a professional after all."

The last of the equipment was placed next to the cot and Toby proceeded to sit on the cold floor to start the assembly process. He had his back to the bikers and focused on the task at hand.

"Don't fuck this up, *cook!*" Niall pointed at the back of Toby's head while imagining pushing a blade into the base of the skull that never turned or showed any reaction whatsoever. The Irishman had taken an instant dislike to Toby for reasons he couldn't quite explain, but he knew all about the madman's reputation. Harrison was confident that they would make a lot of money from the cannibal, which was a good thing, and yet Niall just couldn't connect with the cook. He had an unwashed scrawny hippie vibe about him and an arrogance that just rubbed him up the wrong way.

"Hey!" Harrison barked. Toby slowly turned on the floor to face the giant biker. "Niall's right," he said as he stepped forwards and brought himself up to his full height and size. "Don't fuck this up Toby. We all know you're a mental case, but don't think for one moment that the Grim Union is scared of you. Any fuck-ups and we'll kill you, slowly and extremely painfully," the biker stared hard as he spoke. "Understood?" He almost foamed at the mouth with thoughts of murder and bloodshed, picturing a Roman battlefield in his mind's eye and thrusting a spear deep into Toby's arsehole.

"Don't worry Harrison," Toby casually said as he turned back to continue his task of assembling the goods. "You're working with the best now. Nothing to get heated about."

The inside of Toby's cell was like a Turkish bath house. The steam was thick enough to chew. The tiny slit in the safety glassed window, along with the paper-thin gap at the bottom of the heavy metal door into the room, were the only things allowing any of the steam to escape. It didn't matter to Toby. It had been months now since he had experienced a good cook-up and he was loving being back in the game. The last time he'd worked up a room full of steam like this had been the craziest day of his life and ultimately how he wound up incarcerated in a cell, but that didn't deter him from doing it all over again. The cooking and the killing had not been connected to each other, they just happened to have occurred on the same day. A day filled with hardcore drug abuse in the form of THC, cocaine, psilocybin and lysergic acid diethylamide. Sure, there had probably been some pill-popping too, but he couldn't quite recall all of the details due to the effects of his main ingredients.

Today, Toby was high on the chemical compounds he had to make do with inside prison. The bikers had only been able to supply him with cold medication, so he was forced to go that extra step and separate the ephedrine and pseudoephedrine from the tablets before it was usable. Throughout the cell the OTC medication was mixed with acetone and then set to a low temperature to remove the inert substances. Toby had actually been impressed by the bikers' ability to supply him with some of the more professional items needed to make crystal meth, freeing him from the trouble of using more unsavoury ingredients such as matches, petrol, drain cleaner and tincture of iodine. If he'd had to go the route of concealing the operation from the screws he would have even had to resort to cat litter to act as a filter to conceal the smell. Thankfully he could forego such things and cook in an almost professional lab. He almost felt like he was back to his old self again. There had been a very rough period at the hospital when he first got arrested after the car crash and then the whole ordeal of the court case, followed by his first weeks of sweating and shaking behind bars. But today he was almost back to his old self, high on drugs and cooking yet more drugs. He was back in his element once again.

Toby hadn't quite realised it yet as he had been behaving this way for a number of years now, although not as severely, but he was muttering to himself a lot. As he moved through the fog, spreading pastes, mixing powders and shaking up liquids he spoke incomprehensibly to himself. There were moments when he would suddenly stop at the perceived sight of some long ears or a fluffy tail, but at no point was he consciously trying to communicate with the strange giant rabbits he was unsure if he was actually seeing or not. He pushed past the thoughts when they surfaced and continued to force himself to just concentrate on the cook. Nothing else mattered, only the drugs.

Unbeknownst to the chef, outside his cell the other prisoners were forced to walk by his door with rags placed over their mouths and at a brisk pace. Over the years Toby had become immune to many of the smells and gasses produced from cooking illegal narcotics. Even the new toxins used in his current conditions didn't faze him – he was a professional after all. Sure, he'd tied a T-shirt around the lower part of his face when using the acid because it was a must, but for the most part he didn't even notice the other noxious fumes causing the cons passing by his door to splutter, cough and choke. He wouldn't have cared anyway, even if he had been notified, for the cook must go on.

As the months rolled on and Toby's drugs spread throughout the prison via the Grim Union and corrupt guards, supply met demand and then was almost exceeded by it. Originally Toby had insisted that he would cook it, nothing more, unless you counted consuming it too. Now prisoners were beginning to just turn up at his door to score. Once they had had a taste of what he was making they all wanted some. The Grim Union were unable to meet the demand from the incarcerated drug addicts and would regularly have to tell them to come back in a few days. This caused some to go directly to the source and of course once a few started doing it, more followed. Eventually, there was an almost constant line of prisoners waiting for their turn to enter the steam room and get their next dose.

Toby had initially been angry and demanded that the bikers and guards put an end to it, but both parties had pointed out that it was technically his own fault. If it wasn't so obvious where the shit was being made, the prisoners couldn't have found him. If the shit wasn't so good, they wouldn't want to find him. Eventually Toby relented and just started flogging gear to people as they turned up for whatever they could offer that interested him. Some had cash, others clothes, and inmates offered anything and everything they had in order to score that next trip to escapism. Toby had a steady pile of crap building in his cell, but was unwilling to accept any sexual favours as payment – of which there had been many propositions. All the while he still supplied the bikers and guards the necessary quotas to keep them on side and bringing him what he needed. He still used the same charming and witty sales banter he had always possessed, the kind that made people want to spit in his face or kick it in. His lack of people skills had ensured that he rarely had to deal with the customers on the outside, but in prison it made no difference. Most of the inmates were pretty unsociable themselves, and all were so desperate to get his gear that they didn't give a damn how blunt or rude he was when serving up.

Almost all day every day, a line of prisoners would be stood along the tier where his cell was located and one or two at a time would enter, score, leave and consume. He never had any hassle from anyone, they all loved his gear too much to fuck around and jeopardise missing out on it. And on top of that, they all knew he was associated with and cooking for the Union, who in many ways ran the prison.

At no point was the cook ever stopped or even put on hold. Toby was at it relentlessly day and night. Sleep would be whatever he could get between producing various batches; downtime was when he sat down to mix something; food and water were consumed while cooking. It hadn't taken him long to turn his prison cell into a semi-professional lab, something to rival even his previous set-up at the house.

"What you got?" another prisoner asked from somewhere in the mist.

"Which way you wanna go?" came the chef's curt reply. "Up, down or round the fucking world?"

"Down," said the heavyset man. "I wanna sleep."

The steam before him shifted and Toby's hand appeared holding two green pills.

"Take these," he said. "Make sure you're on your cot before swallowing them." Then his other hand appeared in the grey, open with the palm facing up.

The prisoner placed some folded sterling onto the open hand and then waited until he heard a satisfied grunt before taking the little green sleeping agents from the other. He then turned and hastily exited the sweatbox, wiping his brow and pulling his sticky T-shirt away from his slimy pale flesh. After shouldering his way through the queuing addicts he made it to the top of the stairs leading down to the ground floor. The prisoner tossed the pills into his mouth, tipped his head back and then dry swallowed both of them. It wasn't easy to swallow pills without water, but he was eager to feel their effects and before he could make it halfway down the metal steps he did. The hefty prisoner didn't have time to register what was happening as he immediately slipped into a sound and very deep sleep as he rolled head over heels down the steep metal stairs. When his body crashed to the bottom in a heap on the concrete, he started to make snoring noises and letting off loud farts. Other prisoners in the vicinity and onlookers from above nodded their heads in approval of the drugs. The chef and his products had gained quite the approval rating inside.

Up on high, leaning against the barrier of the third tier, were the Grim Union. They had watched the prisoner fall after popping the downers and were also watching the constant flow of junkies entering and exiting Toby's cell.

"The cook was right," Yago said with a nod.

"Yes, he was," Harrison added with matching nods of approval.

"Is this not a bit too in the guards' fucking faces?" Niall felt like someone had to ask the obvious question.

"Whatever he's giving them seems to be enough for now," Harrison replied while motioning with his head to two guards on the same floor as Toby's cell. Both prison personnel were casually leaning against the barrier, chatting and ignoring the unrelenting line of junkies moving past them. It was clear that from the distance they were standing from the cell they would also be able to smell the noxious fumes that leaked out of it.

"This won't last," Niall grimaced.

It hadn't taken Toby too long to tire of the constant stream of prisoners bothering him while he tried to work. Eventually the inevitable happened and he snapped. The resulting violence caused fear to spread throughout the entire wing. The majority of the populace behind the bars panicked at the thought of the cook ceasing his activities, and many also got an uneasy sack-shrinking sensation when they heard how badly he had hurt the junkie who had bothered him at the wrong time. It was rumoured that Toby had attacked him with some of the hydriodic acid he used for preparing the pseudoephedrine necessary for making meth. Nobody knew for sure what really went down in his cell that day as it had been just before lock-up and most prisoners were already back in their cells riding out their purchased highs and lows. Some had heard the screams, others reckoned they had seen the guards carrying out the victim, but nobody was really certain. All that was known for now was that nobody entered Toby's cell except for the screws and bikers.

It was two greedy guards who had entered today to find Toby walking around his wet-slicked cell completely naked. He checked the sizes of flames and the levels of propane, the consistency of mixes and ignored the new arrivals who closed the door behind them for the privacy required to do what they wanted in peace.

"What's all this then?" the guard with a thick north Wales accent asked mockingly.

"A cook," Toby replied without looking at them or thinking about the fact he was completely naked and lubricious.

"You don't look like no Jamie-fucking-Oliver to me boy," the other guard sounded off in his thick Cockney brogue. "You may be a Naked-fucking-Chef but that don't look like no Sunday roast to me."

"What you cooking boy?" the Welsh guard asked with a wave of his baton in the general direction of the cell.

"Drugs," Toby replied.

"That's illegal," the man said with more mockery. "That's time in the hole," he added with a smile.

"That's you bang in fucking trouble sunshine," his partner

added.

"I made a deal with—"

"Not with us you fucking haven't!" the Cockney yelled, now pointing his baton at Toby who still wandered around not really paying that much attention to them.

"Face the wall and get down on your fucking knees prisoner!" the Welsh guard ordered. "Hands behind your fucking head, fingers interlocked! NOW!" He took a step forwards, baton raised ready to strike with force.

"Don't fuck around boys, this shit is time sensitive and needs my full atten—"

"Do as you're fucking told you cunt!" The Londoner stepped forwards this time.

"Suck my dick!" Toby yelled back while grabbing his sweat-slicked cock and presenting it to the guards like he was about to begin pissing on them.

The guards slowly turned their stern faces to one another and nodded confirmation in unison that they needed to enact the plan they had concocted earlier in the day for such a scenario. The Welshman smiled widely at Toby while retrieving something from his pocket with his free hand, all the while distracting the cook from paying attention to his partner opening the cell door. The Welsh screw then screamed loudly in a battle cry of rage as he took another step toward Toby, who was armed only with his small and greasy sex organ, and then proceeded to spray tear gas into his face at a very close distance before quickly exiting the cell. His partner slammed the heavy door closed behind him once he was safely out and on the landing. The two guards chuckled from behind the safety of the now locked cell door while lighting cigarettes and listening to the sounds of Toby screaming, spluttering, howling and coughing.

By the time they had finished smoking all sounds from within Toby's cell had ceased. They opened the hatch to check what he was doing before entering again. Toby was standing against the far wall, his forehead pressed against its wet surface. He didn't move or make any sound. The guards closed the hatch and entered the cell, figuring he was still partially blind and trying to recover from the spraying he'd received. Before the guards could make it even halfway into the cell, Toby span around and threw something in their faces. Neither would ever know for sure what it was. The rumours would later circulate around the prison that it was Toby's weapon of choice: hydriodic acid. Other rumours would circulate that he bit their faces off. All the two guards knew for sure in that moment of time was that it burnt worse than anything they'd ever experienced before. It was the kind of pain that made you wish for death. The kind that didn't let you pass out, but instead kept you just on the brink between madness and blackness.

Toby dragged the screaming screws out of his cell while still completely naked, muttering incoherently to himself. He could have been dragging common household rubbish out he did it so nonchalantly. After he'd dumped the screaming human waste on the cold grate of the landing he turned and went back into his cell to continue cooking, closing the door behind him.

From inside their locked cells, the entire wing listened to the horrifying screams of the two guards whose faces would never be the same again. The prisoners close enough could also here Toby say, "Shut the fuck up! I'm trying to concentrate in here!" followed   by   atonal   whistling.

The entire wing felt like it was going to start rumbling and shaking from the sight of so many guards fully kitted out in tactical riot gear bearing giant shields. The sound of their heavy boots stomping the concrete and metal flooring as they travelled from the main entrance up to the first floor was deafening. There were only 20 of them led by warden Theodore Rinckel dressed in his usual grey suit and white shirt, but the noise they made created the impression of an entire army storming through.

They all made a b-line straight for Toby's cell without pausing or stopping for anything, including his cell door. The warden was first in and surrounded by his private militia immediately, all ready for whatever fight the chemist would put up against them.

Theodore felt like Patton charging into battle with his troops, ready to vanquish evil. That illusion was met with the harsh reality of the fumes being produced by the current batch of crystal meth Toby was working on. The acidic gasses filled the nostrils and eyes of the warden and he started to cough and splutter due to the lack of protection against the chemicals. Mr Rinckel wasn't sure if Patton ever had to go up against any kind of chemical warfare but he was sure it would have stopped him in his tracks had he faced what was currently infusing his chubby chops.

Past the chemical fumes the guards could see Toby dancing naked and off his nut on whatever cocktail of narcotics he had already consumed in preparation for their arrival. He paid them no mind as he waved his bare arse to the sounds of his own horrid voice singing not only off-key, but minus rhythm and at a pitch that even dogs couldn't hear without howling in pain. He stopped wailing to take another hit on the glass pipe in his hand as he turned to face the mini army now crowding into his cell. The warden was doubled over, teary eyed and struggling to breathe. He looked up just in time to catch a giant waft of methamphetamine smoke blown into his already hurting features. He coughed and was suddenly hoisted backwards by his elbows and passed through the rank of guards until he landed out on the tier into what passed as fresh air in the prison. Toby paid none of it any mind, he continued to strut, swing his bits and smoke his crystal as he cooked on.

"What in the fucking hell is going on in there?!" squawked Theodore between gasps for air.

"A cook!" Toby yelled back while readying for another hit on his pipe. "I'm busy so piss off!" He managed to get one last final suck on the pipe before the wall of shields smashed into him and a flurry of batons came hammering down.

The warden stepped aside and patted his eyes dry to the sight of an unconscious Toby being hauled away by his men. A wave of black, like giant ants marching forth from their nest, carried Toby away and off the wing. Theodore stood tall on the first floor tier and smiled triumphantly at the sight.

The tunnel was in almost complete darkness until he reached the single bare bulb suspended outside the barred hole in the wall. Harrison had spent several years in this prison and had been incarcerated in several others over the course of his life of crime, but he'd never seen a cell like the one he saw now. It was like something from a medieval dungeon rather than a 21st-century prison. A small cave set into a wall deep below the ground, with thick bars separating it from a dirty tunnel that had never seen sunlight. To the biker it was worse than the hole they used for solitary confinement. Sure that was bad, but it at least had the look of nothing more than a plain box. Nothing sinister. This place felt like it was designed to drive you insane. To make you feel like you were the only living creature left in existence, all alone in darkness or occasionally illuminated by the single bulb that didn't appear to be stronger than 10 watts. The damp and dirt added to the gothic feel and amplified the grim desolation.

Inside the cell he saw the naked and shivering body of Toby laying on the thread-thin piss-stained mattress they'd supplied him with. This too looked like it was made during the times of kings and castles. There was nothing else in the cell as far as Harrison could make out. He assumed there were buckets or holes somewhere for the prisoner to piss and shit in, but he couldn't see anything just smell it.

"Hey," the bodybuilder said through the bars he now casually leaned against, "cook."

Toby lay and shivered in silence.

"Too bad, Toby. It was good while it lasted—"

In the blink of an eye Toby leapt from the mattress and onto the bars that separated him from Harrison and the tunnel. He gripped the cold and filthy metal like a demented ape, naked, bloody, beaten and bruised all over. He looked like something from a horror film. A freak of nature gone horribly wrong and abandoned by fortune.

"It's not over Harrison!" Toby managed to blurt through his busted lips "The cook mustn't end!" he spluttered.

Harrison stepped back out of arms' reach and smiled softly, "The warden thinks differently."

"It's just a temporary setback," the crank was all that kept him going now and also fuelled his delusional mind. "Bring all the shit down here. Sure, the ventilation is a little bit shit but—"

"It's done," the mountain of muscle said firmly to the pale white specimen clinging to the bars before him. "Maybe we can do something else in the future, *Casper*. Until then, perhaps you should think about getting yourself clean." Harrison nodded as a sign of respect to the cook and then turned and walked away into the blackness to the sounds of Toby howling.

Chapter 3 – Past

Amsterdamned

The train ride into Centraal went smoothly. Mark and Toby had slid into a relatively busy carriage and sat among the passengers mainly made up of commuters going into whatever nine-to-five gig they had going on alongside fresh-faced tourists straight off the plane. Mark and Toby were neither, as they had just been stowaways on public transport as well as the guilty parties responsible for several stolen cars from France's western coast to the train they currently sat on without tickets. They kept their heads down and eyes open for any conductors while being mostly ignored by the other travellers.

The pair looked malnourished, in desperate need of a good wash and few days' sleep. If it wasn't for their skin colour, it would have just been assumed by the other passengers that they were Middle Eastern refugees and not the two escaped British felons that they were. Of course, nobody knew that they were actually on the run as the news hadn't been of any interest to the media outside of the UK.

The two illegals strutted casually out of the station and straight down the main strip – Damrak. They ignored all of the eateries and bars – neither had any cash so there was no point in even looking.

"Time for a new start my friend," Toby said in an unusually chipper tone.

Mark tried to recall if he had ever heard Toby speak that merrily before and couldn't. Considering all they had been through lately, it was unusual for his friend to sound optimistic, but then they had just arrived in what Toby had always referred to as the land of milk and honey. Or, to be more accurate, the land of weed and hash. Toby had always wanted to move to Amsterdam and open his own coffee shop, he even had a name for it – The Atom Café. Mark had often said that the Welsh Assembly would have been a more fitting name, considering they were natives of Cymru. Toby had never cared much about patriotism and always insisted that his love of science came before all else, except drugs of course – that went without saying. Mark had always found it ironic and slightly annoying that someone who hated religion and religious people as much as

Toby did because of their blind faith had an almost dogmatic adherence to science, despite the fact that so much of it was still just classed as theory and was often altered or thrown out as old and not matching with current findings, which weren't always to be trusted as they may well have been paid for by biased patrons out with an agenda.

"A new start. I hope you're right dude," Mark said. His tone let Toby know that he still wasn't convinced that his plan would work.

"Trust me, the Union know what I'm capable of." Toby had already told Mark all about the operation he had set up inside prison with the bikers and that he had their respect after what he had accomplished with so little. "We just have to find them first."

That was the one flaw in Toby's plan as far as Mark could tell. In all the time he'd been locked up with the biker outlaws, at no point had they mentioned or he enquired where their clubhouse was. He knew their founding chapter was located somewhere in Amsterdam because Lars had mentioned it in passing one day. But that was all he knew – no more, no less. And as well as he knew the city, Amsterdam was still a pretty big place to search.

Mark and Toby drifted around central Amsterdam and spent a lot of time gawping at the windows in the Red Light district. Toby couldn't remember the last time he had been with a woman and Mark was starting to feel the same way. Sure, for Toby it was normal, but for a player like Mark it was a strange thing to not know with any kind of certainty when he would be having sex again. Deep down he knew when the last time he had it was and pushed the depressing memory back into his subconscious. Toby was also having depressing recollections of how long it had been since he did something: smoke a spliff. Every street was laced with the fragrant perfume of his favourite thing in the world and he couldn't get any of it because they were skint. He almost had to fight back the tears.

After hours of wandering around the canals, streets, narrow alleys and anywhere else their exhausted feet carried them they eventually came to a canal-side road lined with the usual apartments and businesses, but with one glaring exception. This street had an extremely rowdy bar on it with over a dozen giant motorcycles all lined up outside. As the pair ventured closer they noticed a short fat biker step outside and light a cigarette before taking out his phone and making a call. As he smoked and talked he casually approached one of the hogs and then swung a denim leg over it and straddled the black leather seat. His back now facing Mark and Toby, it was clear that the lower rocker on his leather waistcoat read 'Amsterdam,' but more importantly the top one read 'The Grim Union' and the insignia between them was a familiar image that Toby had seen tattooed on the flesh of the bikers he'd been locked up with – two skeletal hands making fists and pointing up as a sign of power, one white and one black, behind a jawless skull.

"Fuckin' bingo," Toby said with a smile and a nod.

Mark and Toby both stopped on the other side of the street overlooking the canal and took in the sights and sounds of the place. It had a very typical American biker bar vibe, the kind they'd seen in movies and on TV but never in real life. Loud heavy metal and raucous voices, saloon doors and some buzzing neon lighting. They both thought it looked kind of cliched and obvious. There was no name above the entrance, but clearly it was not for the casual drinker or tourist and therefor no signage or advertising was necessary.

"So, let me get this straight," Mark said with clear apprehension. "You're doing all the talking, right?"

"Yep," Toby replied with confidence.

"*Not* me," Mark said with obvious signs of still being confused with his partner's plan.

"They don't know you," Toby restated the same argument he had put up earlier when having the same exact conversation with Mark.

"*Still*," Mark really wanted to change Toby's mind about doing all of the talking. When they had dealt drugs together in the past the agreement had always been that Mark was the salesman and Toby was the cook. They had always been in complete and utter agreement that Toby's people skills were pretty much extinct. "You're not exactly Nas when it comes to word play," Mark said as he recalled how many times customers had threatened to kill Toby because of something he had said, which was usually a direct insult spat at them with nothing but naked contempt. "I can't help but think you're gonna say something to piss them off." Mark really did not want to have his life ended in a biker bar after all they had been through simply because Toby made some derogatory remark about them all wearing leather or someone sporting a pair of chaps. "You do have a history."

"Relax," Toby reassured his friend. "I'm sure Harrison will have told them about me and the sweet deal we had going on inside." This was what it all came down to in the end. Mark knew that outlaw bikers weren't about to entertain the thought of speaking to him, a complete unknown, but Toby had served time with some of their highest-ranking members.

"But..." Mark didn't want to offend Toby. They'd been on the road for what felt like months and were both too tired for petty squabbles or full-blown arguments. Besides, they had a mission to accomplish that would either save their lives or condemn them to being adrift in Amsterdam until they perished from exposure or starvation or frustration. There was no backup plan or alternative strategy to survive. It was all or nothing: hook up with the bikers.

"But what?"

"You're shit with people," Mark had to remind his friend of the obvious. "You can't negotiate," he restated his previous argument. "Every sales pitch I've ever heard you make ended in violence."

"I'm a changed man," Toby announced sternly with a raised palm in his partner's face. And with that, Toby was walking away, across the road and straight toward the biker bar.

Mark followed reluctantly. He knew there was no other way to go about this and yet he still felt like he should be the one doing the majority of the talking. He had tried to persuade Toby to just casually make their way into the bar and be the initial opener of the conversation. Mark should be the one to do most of the legwork and final closing remarks. Toby had argued that it must be him doing all the talking, as he was the one they knew of, and more importantly knew they could trust him because of his history of doing time with their brother bikers.

The inside of the Grim Union's biker bar was everything Mark and Toby had expected it to be from the outside. Dark, loud, smoky and full of big men covered in denim and leather and scars and tattoos. Some were big because of muscles, but most were just fat. Toby could see that serving time in prison was actually a healthier option for outlaw bikers, as the ones he met inside were all ripped and jacked.

Their boots and trainers stuck to the threadbare carpet as they made their way through the looks of confusion and hostility to the bar that ran parallel to the left wall. The burly bikers who noticed the out-of-place duo lowered their beers and glared at the two men who were clearly not members of the club, bikers or indeed outlaws. Of course, the last assumption was wrong – technically very wrong. Mark and Toby most certainly were outlaws, but they just didn't feel the need to wear it advertised on a leather jacket or start an all-boys club to promote the fact that they were escaped prisoners wanted by the long arm of the British law.

The further the two walked into the bar the more people stared at them. Mark was just waiting for someone to stop the music by dragging the needle across the vinyl to make that unpleasant scratching sound. The thrash metal never stopped or got turned down, but he did notice a drop in the amount of raucous laughter emanating from the patrons and background chatter that had been prevalent when they'd first walked in. Mark tried not to make eye contact with any of the people he passed, be it biker, bodybuilder, metal head or skanky female sporting Daisy Dukes and bruises from where they'd been put in their place for speaking out of turn. Sure, Mark knew that most of the men not wearing patches would have to be associated with the club in some way or another just to be allowed to drink there, but they still looked like they belonged in that almost pitch-black watering hole. By comparison, Mark and Toby looked like drag queens in a mosque.

At the bar they were met by a very confused barman in his fifties sporting a spiderweb tattoo over the top of his shaved head.

"Who's the top dog?" Toby asked immediately with an arrogant confidence that even made Mark want to slap him.

"The what?" the Dutch native asked, still clearly confused.

"Top dog," Toby replied condescendingly. "Head honcho," he spoke like the barman was deaf and dumb. "Numero uno," he included sign language to add further affront to the insulting tone of voice. "El Capitan," he beat his palm on the bar impatiently. "The motherfucking kingpin," Mark died a little inside with every shit expression out of his dumb partner's mouth. "He who must be obeyed," Toby concluded with a look that said it was blatantly obvious what he wanted and the barman must be a bloody idiot for not understanding him, but he just stared at Toby with no idea what was going on or what the strange little hippie wanted.

"We're looking to get with the club president," Mark leaned in and said casually.

The barman nodded confirmation that he both understood and could help. He walked away into the darkness away from the main entrance.

"Don't fuck this up," Mark said out of the side of his mouth to Toby, trying to say it quietly enough so that nobody else in the vicinity would hear or notice any tension between them.

"Not my fault the twat doesn't understand English," Toby blurted out at full volume.

At the far end of the bar they watched the barman lean over and talk into the ear of a late-twenties giant. Luuk was young but he had earned a big reputation in his native Holland among both criminal and biker fraternities as someone not to fuck with. His size, coupled with his skills and speed with his fists, had quickly got him not only a patch with the Grim, but also a position as one of their top enforcers. Luuk liked violence and he was good at it, and this is something the biker gang needed and respected. After the barman had informed him of Mark and Toby's presence, as well as their desire to speak to a ranking member of the club, he put his beer down on the bar and approached the pair of idiots who clearly didn't belong in such an establishment.

"Yes?" Luuk asked as soon as he was next to Mark and Toby.

"We—" Toby began in a cocky manner with his skinny chest pushed out.

"—We should speak in private," Mark quickly said something sensible and in a level tone.

Toby took offence to this and stared at Mark like he had just spat in his Coco Pops.

"Who are you?" asked the biker.

"My friend did time with some of the Union," Mark continued speaking while Toby continued to stare daggers into the side of his head. "Back in Britain."

Luuk eyed Toby up and down, not seeing anything obvious about the dirty and hairy hippie that would attract his brother bikers to do business with him. Sure, most of his closest friends were dirty and hairy, but they were also big and mean too. Toby looked more like the kind of prisoner the Grim Union boys would victimise and force to wear a miniskirt than actually do time with.

Toby had stopped staring at Mark to regard Luuk, trying his best to make eye contact and show no signs of fear or allowing himself to be alpha-dogged. Toby narrowed his eyes and stuck his jaw out in an attempt to look angry, but of course just wound up looking like he belonged at the back of a special-ed bus.

"Come," Luuk said while nodding his head. As far as he was concerned nobody would lie about doing time with the Union, which meant he should listen to what they had to say in private. If there was any bullshit, he could simply shoot them with the semi-auto he had tucked into his waistband – not a problem.

Luuk led the way deeper into the bar towards some dimly lit pool tables where he could see another enforcer for the club, Levi, and a fully patched member, Jacob, racking the balls for another game. He tapped each of them on the shoulder as he passed without stopping, and both bikers knew to cease what they were doing and follow. While Levi was a fellow Dutchman, Jacob was English and Luuk figured it would be worth having a fellow Brit in the room to ensure no misunderstandings due to the language barrier. Sure, he and Levi were fluent English speakers, but sometimes things were said that could be missed or taken the wrong way.

The back room held a small stage with a strippers' pole at the centre and was surrounded by seats and another long bar parallel to the left wall. This room was also soundproofed due to how rowdy it got sometimes. This made it convenient for conducting business where bullets may end up doing the negotiating. During the day it was almost always empty and unused for legitimate purposes, but at night it was a den of debauchery for bikers, criminals and animals alike. Mark could smell the sex and debauchery in the air as soon as he entered the room, which stirred up old feelings of his past self when he did business from his house and ploughed through women like a farmer late for harvest offerings.

Luuk stood before the stage, flanked by his fellow bikers, and crossed his giant arms over his gorilla-sized chest. Mark and Toby stood before him and wished they could take a rest.

"Who'd you do time with?" the biker asked.

"The Grim Union," Toby answered condescendingly. "Weren't you listening?" His old people skills had resurfaced immediately, much to Mark's disappointment, which he openly showed with his hung head and a loud sigh. "What?!" Again Toby was offended by his partner's attitude.

"Their names numb nuts!" Mark said exasperated.

"Oh, yeah," Toby now realised his error, "Harrison, Niall—"

"You did time with Harrison?" Luuk asked in shock. Harrison was one of the top riders in the club and a legend for all he had done in its name.

Toby nodded affirmation and was unimpressed with the biker's tone of voice. It had an air of disbelief that suggested Toby wasn't man enough to have done time with Harrison.

"What you want with us?" Luuk asked.

"Same deal as with Harrison," Toby said. He didn't say any more as he fully expected Luuk to not only know who he was, but what deal he had struck. Luuk, of course, had no idea who Toby was or what he had going on with Harrison.

"Which is…?" Mark quietly prompted his partner.

"Don't you remember?" Toby replied. "I told you before

dude."

"For fuck's sake Toby!" Mark yelled in disbelief, and with a feeling of crushing exhaustion he said very slowly and deliberately, "I know, but they don't. So tell them you twat!"

All three bikers were now on edge and figured that this was some weird strategy by the two homeless-looking guys to get them alone and separated from the rest of the club in order to rob or kill them. Luuk pictured where the grip of his pistol was and started to consider pulling the piece out as a warning to the strangers.

"What the fuck is this about Luuk?" asked Jacob, who was confused and in no mood for bullshit. Luuk could only shrug his shoulders.

"Fuck it!" Mark yelled unexpectedly. He knew he had to take charge of the situation and do the talking before the bikers let their fists and possibly guns do the talking. "My partner cooked gear for the Union on the inside. He was supplying Harrison and his boys for a while, before the warden closed it down and threw him in the dungeon." Mark pointed at Toby.

"You're... *the cook*?" asked an astonished Levi.

Toby's chest, head and cock swelled up at the realisation that the biker knew who he was. The legend of the cook had obviously preceded him across the channel and into Europe – Amsterdam, the stoner centre of the continent no less. He truly was a living legend.

Mark could sense the ego emanating out of his partner. He didn't even need to look at him to know that he would have an ear-to-ear grin and an erection at the knowledge that hardcore gangsters in another country had heard of him. It seemed pretty obvious to Mark that the bikers would have heard of him considering he'd been cooking for members of the club, but he knew his attention-starved partner-in-crime would read a whole lot more into it.

"You know who I am!" Toby blurted out with joy. He knew that Harrison and the others must have informed their fellow bikers of how he had been a narcotic alchemist behind bars, knocking up cream from crap in his cell and supplying the whole prison with drugs that had them coming back in droves for more day after day.

"Niall said he's a fuckin' lunatic," Levi informed Luuk with a shake of the head that signalled he had only heard bad things about the legendary Welsh cook.

"You're Casper," said Jacob.

Toby almost came in his dirty pants.

"I'm a fucking legend!" the cook screamed at the top of his lungs. "Inter-fucking-nationally known mofo!" Toby got up into Mark's face like an MMA fighter talking shit to a lesser opponent during a press conference. "Superstar biatch!" He threw two Nixonesque peace signs in the air before letting out a Michael Jackson-like scream and thrusting his crotch at Mark, who merely stood and stared unimpressed with his graceless friend.

"I never heard of you," Luuk said flatly.

"Likewise big boy" Toby said over his shoulder without missing a beat.

Even before Luuk had balled his giant hands into rock-hard fists Mark was turning and ready to run for the door. He wasn't sure if he would make it out alive, and even less sure that his idiot partner would, but every molecule of his being told him that he had to escape before the giant mound of muscle wrapped in leather and denim forced him to watch Toby being fisted to death.

"Hold up a second Luuk," Jacob informed him before he finished taking that first step towards killing the chef. "Word has it the fella cooked top shit with next to nothing behind bars."

"Can you make speed?" Asked Levi.

"I can make fucking magic," Toby said cockily. "I can turn night into day," he said while doing a little shoulder shake and head slide. "I can send you round the Sun and to the Moon and back," he swirled his finger around in the air. "I can—"

"Can you cook crank? We need speed," the biker asked again.

"What did I—"

"Yes," Mark saved his partner one more time, "he can cook speed. Great speed. And meth – the best you've ever blazed or shot up." Mark stepped forwards to block Toby from the bikers, a physical manoeuvre to hopefully send signals to his friend's subconscious to shut the fuck up for a moment. "Top shit no problem. On time, on price and on weight," he slipped back into his old salesman ways. "Give him a kitted-out kitchen and the ingredients and he'll cook it to whatever strength you want it." Mark raised his eyebrows and nodded assurance that his claims were true.

"I need to speak to Harrison," Luuk said. "I need to be sure you're for real."

"Cool," Mark said with another nod before Toby could say something stupid and potentially lethal.

"Go have a drink," Luuk continued. "I'll make some calls." He then nodded at his fellow bikers who escorted Mark and Toby back out to the bar as he fished his phone out of his pocket and began   dialling.

Mark and Toby knew that they would be starting off small even before the bikers had said it out loud, but this was something else. The tower block was located in the arse-end of some dreary Amsterdam suburb and still had the remnants of whatever rectum had shat it forth all over its facade and dripping within. Every building looked like it had survived a recent war or riot, barely, and was now tagged with crude graffiti by the victors. There were more empty windows than there were with panes of glass. The black holes of the vacant windows all around them looked like a thousand lifeless giant eyes staring down and asking that question nobody wants to hear when you've wandered into the wrong part of town: *what you doing round here then?* Mark and Toby were asking themselves this very same question. They both knew the answer could basically be boiled down to one word: desperation. The pair had fled the UK and its authorities, both legitimate and clandestine, without a penny between them. To get this far they had stolen whatever necessity had been required, just like true desperados.

Now, stood in a semi-derelict flat facing several members of an international criminal organisation known for loving motorbikes and extreme violence, Mark and Toby wanted to protest at what they were being offered, but both knew better. Well, at least Mark did.

"What the fuck is this shithole?!" Toby exclaimed as he pointed randomly around the empty room, which gave a clear view of most of the other rooms in the flat. They were on the top floor of a building that they had been assured was safe to cook in due to the lack of tenants. Mark remembered what Toby had said as they left Centraal: 'Time for a new start my friend' and here it was: their very own smashed-up trap-house. Most people had left the neighbourhood years ago due to a lack of resources and police presence. The bikers had taken over several buildings for all intents and purposes, but didn't officially own a square inch. Nothing on paper, but anyone left squatting or hiding in the tower blocks knew that the Grim Union ran this end of town now.

The flat had no glass in any of the windows and the only

frame that still held a door was the main entrance, which Mark realised was enforced by a large steel plate and several deadbolts. Many of the walls had giant holes smashed through them or were no longer standing. For the most part there was just the main shell and supporting walls still in place. Bare concrete throughout gave it an even more depressing vibe, and the whole place was covered in dirt and grime. The sockets and light fittings were mostly just more holes, some with the occasional wire dangling from it.

"Where you will cook," answered Bram Jansen. "And live." The Grim Union club secretary was in his early fifties and looked like Marvel's The Thing, only less human-looking.

"What? This-this-thi—"

Bram held up one of his giant and lined hands to silence Toby. The secretary's look spelled a lack of interest in hearing any shit from the cook, or indeed anyone else for that matter. It was obvious from both the expression on his face and the tone of his voice that Bram simply did not fuck around and had probably never been born with or acquired a sense of humour.

"You provide me a list of whatever: equipment and ingredients," he explained in an almost monotone voice to Toby. "I will get, then you cook."

Despite being Dutch, Mark couldn't help but think that Bram must have some Russian blood in him. He had a very old-school commie way about him, the kind you saw in Hollywood movies when they did historical flicks that demonised the Ruskies. "Is there a toilet at least?" Mark asked, figuring the answer would involve the word 'bucket.'

"We'll bring extra buckets," Luuk said with a nod.

This was the final piece of evidence that Mark needed to confirm his theory that the bikers were going to fuck them for as much as they could. He knew that they would exploit himself and Toby like a couple of trafficked slaves.

"Did Harrison not tell you who I am and what I can fucking do?!" Toby yelled at Bram, who showed no reaction.

"He said you're very good," Luuk answered. "He also said you're a fucking..." the bodybuilder trailed off as he tried to remember the exact words Harrison had used to describe Toby. "'…a complete fucking lunatic and giant liability.'" Luuk stopped and then after a moment nodded conformation that he had remembered the description accurately enough. "Yes, something like this."

"Sounds about right," Mark said while looking at his dishevelled partner.

"We start small," Bram announced. "You do good, we grow and give you more. Speed first, yes?" And with that Bram took out a small notepad and pen that he handed to Toby. As he began to write down everything he would need he started walking around the barren shell they would be calling both their workspace and home for God knows how long.

The bare concrete walls had water cascading down them in only one part of the flat. Despite having no glass in the windows to restrict the steam from the cook escaping, and despite the cold Dutch temperature up on the top floor of the high-rise block, Toby and Mark had still managed to turn yet another improvised space into a sweaty chemical sauna.

Toby now had multiple homemade set-ups all over the place for mixing chemicals, heating others and grinding up pills. He knew that the quality of the powder would depend on this mixing of chemicals in such a small space, as well as the methods he was reduced to, but as far as he was concerned the product would still be better than anything the bikers had ever come across before. "So fuck them," he muttered. He was all about quantity not quality until the bikers improved their living and working conditions. Originally, he and Mark had been pissed about the state of the flat but when they started having to resort to the old school shake-and-bake method of cooking they were glad of the open air flow system thanks to the missing panes in the window frames.

They'd been at it for weeks now, cooking constantly. In one corner of the flat, close to the barricaded front door, lay a big mound of little Ziploc baggies filled with speed ready to punt out to the end user. The bikers would turn up every few days and collect the baggies in panniers, rucksacks or whatever other means they wanted to use to gather the merchandise. There would be little to no conversation when members of the Grim Union turned up. The bikers had all decided that the duo were not worth talking to as they were constantly fucked out of their nuts on their own product. Mark and Toby had no cash to buy weed or any other drugs due to the bikers not paying them yet, so they smoked a shit-load of the meth they produced and just worked constantly day and night. They had both lost all track of time or even the meaning of the concept of time. Life for the pair of them consisted of nothing more than cooking speed and smoking crystal methamphetamine.

As the weeks turned into months, the flat developed from simply being a shell with a shake-and-bake operation inside it into what is commonly referred to in the illicit industry as a Beavis-and-Butt-Head lab until it eventually almost looked like a high-end facility. Sure, a lot of the equipment was still low-tech but the laboratory had expanded and the place even had electricity, running water, countless propane tanks and new glass in the windows. Toby had also managed to convince the bikers they should start investing in some real glassware, such as beakers, pipettes and Mason jars. It had been almost inconceivable to Toby in the beginning that a criminal enterprise like the Grim Union would even bother to try and set-up shop without investing more than a couple of euros into the equipment, but that's how it went.

Much to Mark's delight the bikers had eventually provided them with a real toilet. Unfortunately he and Toby had to plumb it in as the bikers had merely dumped it outside the door and then fucked off. Toby hadn't cared much about having a toilet as he had got used to using buckets back in prison and had even taken to simply pissing and shitting off the balcony of the tower block on days where the temperature wasn't too harsh on his genitals. Along with the toilet and better lab equipment the bikers had brought them cots and a sound system. Sure, it was just an old CD player and the CDs provided were various forms of metal, but when flying off your face on crank the guttural screams and feedback   suited   them.

Before a full year had ended the flat had transformed into something resembling their old operation back in Wales. The place was now fitted out with internal doors, walls and even comfortable furniture. Different rooms had now been equipped to manufacture or grow different narcotics, each with functional extraction systems to remove the stink.

Mark and Toby now stood in what had become their joint favourite enterprise. It was flooded with powerful lights and housed row upon row of bushy green plants. The cannabis buds were almost touching the LED lamps – Toby had really gone for it and grown them with steroid-like strength. Mark was impressed, but of course would never say or show it to his friend.

"Look out Superman," Toby said with a broad smile, "Kryptonite is making a comeback!" He almost jumped out of his skin with excitement at the prospect of yet again getting his lips on a big fat spliff of his old favourite strain. They'd been getting some money from the bikers for a while and using it to go out and smoke gear, but nothing in Amsterdam had ever come close to what Toby truly desired. Mark had suggested they start growing another strain months ago, but Toby had insisted that they wait until he could find the right seeds to cross pollinate and develop his devastating super skunk with. They had agreed not to mention it to the bikers – this was just for them for the time being.

In the back room of the biker bar all five members of the Grim Union committee were in attendance, along with another 10 of the main members and two prospects who were close to becoming fully-fledged Grims. They were a mixed European bunch, but the leaders had always been of Dutch or British origins. It had never been planned that way, it just happened. The club had started in the Netherlands and so of course it was inevitable that key members would be Dutch. How the Brits got so involved was no different to how any of the other nationalities got on board; it just happened. If you were a rider and a criminal, you stood a reasonable chance of getting in.

The bikers all sat around the tables, sipping beers and smoking a variety of cigarettes and spliffs. Some were high (or low) on other substances too, but at the moment there was just drinking and smoking going on in the back bar. The only ones not drinking or smoking were the two prospects, Stijn and Andras, as they were on service duty for the committee while the meeting was on.

Stood before the biker committee were Mark and Toby, both still showing the effects of all the crank they'd been consuming. Even after the operation had taken off and the pair had other drugs to take they had continued consuming meth in high doses in order to supply the bikers with vast quantities of the stuff. Sleep and nourishment were usually forgotten about and replaced by more gear going in and going out.

At the centre table sat an ageing man with a long grey beard and ponytail, Vlad 'The Mountain' van de Berg – the president of the Grim Union biker club. The Mountain wasn't just the president of the Amsterdam chapter, he was also the head of the Grim Union worldwide. Back when he had first become a member of the club his height and broad shoulders had earned him the moniker of 'The Mountain,' but now in comparison to some of the other riders in his club he was almost average-looking in physical size. Over time the name had started to be attributed to another quality the criminal possessed – his unwillingness to move on any decision he had set his mind to. At no point did he ever use his own nickname or consider it accurate due to the difference in his physical stature when compared to other members, such as Luuk or Kong.

Kong was the club's sergeant-at-arms and nobody had ever learned what his real name was. The bikers just started calling him Kong on account of him being built like the movie gorilla King Kong. The biker wasn't black or particularly hairy and so there was no worry of the name being taken the wrong way and someone losing their life for being considered a racist by the living breathing giant. Nobody had ever heard Kong speak, which added to the animalistic undertone to him, he simply grunted and stared at people in-between ripping their arms out of their sockets. Nobody knew for sure if the stories were bullshit or not, but he'd allegedly made it his main form of punishing other prisoners while locked up in Holland. Word had got back to the Union that their man was a stone-cold psychopath who was ripping other prisoner's arms off and then beating them with it. A lot of the bikers took this as nothing more than tall tales, but some only had to look at his gigantic physique and figure that maybe, just maybe, it was possible for him to pull off such a feat of strength.

"Business is good," Vlad said with a slight curl of his lips. "You cook fast, you grow fast," the curl stretched further up and across his weathered face. "Good money. Good business," the smile widened and he nodded. "This is good. It is time to go bigger, yes?" It was obviously a rhetorical question aimed at Mark and Toby who he looked down upon as nothing more than slave workers for the club.

"About fu—"

"Yes," Mark cut his partner off before he could finish saying anything that may, and probably would, insult the head of the bikers. "We're good to go."

"Only he cooks though, yes?" Vlad said to Mark while pointing at Toby.

"Yeah," Mark nodded. "I'm more like an assistant in the kitchen. The sous-chef if you like." He realised something was coming that he probably wouldn't like, but the bikers knew how the operation worked and so there was no talking his way around it.

"No more kitchen work for you," Vlad stated bluntly. "We will give the cook all the help he needs in his new kitchen. We have many useful hands."

"Rumour has it you're good behind a wheel," said Danny 'Shooter' Ross, the club's vice president and British influence on the leadership of the biker gang.

Mark answered by way of a slight nod.

"From now on you'll run guns and shift gear for us," Danny said in that way people do when they're not giving you a choice. "Cool?"

Mark simply nodded again. He knew full well that even if he didn't think it was cool, he had to do it anyway or face an alternative that he would like even less.

"No questions?" the slender VP asked.

Mark took a moment to think about this. He'd spent about a year in the UK driving for criminals when he had nothing better to do with his life and had been happy to let it come to an end. Then he'd driven briefly for The French Connection without being given much of a choice. Now he was being made to drive again for another criminal enterprise. While Mark didn't like being made to do things against his will, the truth was he fucking loved driving fast and got a giant thrill out of highspeed chases with the law. None of the cops in the UK had ever really come close to busting him except for the fat one The French Connection had shot in the face and then set them up for. Sure, the fat man hadn't been much of a driver, but his persistence had made for an interesting chase or two. Maybe, just maybe somewhere on the European continent Mark would meet a copper who could give him a real chase. Someone as skilled behind the wheel as he was and that could offer him up a challenge on the road. Getting off his nut while helping Toby cook was fine, but driving was where it was really at for Mark. A head full of speed while kicking it in a high-speed pursuit sounded fantastic to Mark right now after being cooped up in the flat cooking almost 24/7 with the less-than-hygienic partner of his. So, did he mind being forced to drive guns and gear around

Europe for the bikers? No, not particularly. The only real question was, "Can I choose my ride?" which he asked with a raised eyebrow.

"You'll have something plain," answered Lucas Visser, the club treasurer. "Discreet," the short pot-bellied man said as he peered over his spectacles. "Just a regular car. Nothing that stands ou—"

"I prefer American muscle," Mark cut in. "'Regular' just ain't my style." He gave the middle-aged biker a smile.

"You need to avoid getting stopped," VP Danny said with a sigh. He liked Mark's attitude toward power and speed in a vehicle but this was business.

"Stopping ain't my style either," Mark informed the bikers like it was just a straight-up fact rather than a cocky boast.

"Maybe the stories are true," a Welsh accent spoke up from another table. Mark turned and smiled at a young biker with a shaved head who had introduced himself as Owen. "You should give him something proper to drive Danny," Owen said to the VP. While Owen wasn't a committee member, he was one of the club's enforcers and his opinion was respected. "We've all heard the same rumours," he added with smile shot in Mark's direction.

Danny slowly turned to Bram, who as club secretary would be arranging the vehicle for their new mule to be using, and raised two questioning eyebrows.

"I   see   what   I   can   do,"   Bram   said.

When Mark saw the car he couldn't hold back. He had always been the calm one in the partnership, but now he felt and heard himself doing a 'Toby' when he suddenly blurted out, "What the fuck is that?!"

Stood either side of him, Danny and Bram had expected this reaction, but as far as they were concerned this was a good choice for the tasks they wanted him to complete. All three were stood next to a black BMW 5 Series parked up at one of the club's many garages. Mark had never been a big fan of BMWs – sure they could shift, but the problem he had with this particular motor was, "It's a fucking touring car!" He couldn't believe his eyes. "It's got more arse than Kim Kardashian!" He stepped back and put his hands against the sides of his head. For days he'd been looking forward to sliding behind the wheel of a slick beast tuned to perfection, and now here he stood looking at what was in his opinion a suburban family wagon. Okay, beamers could move and the 5 series were monsters, but this was a touring car not a 'get me the fuck away from the police' car.

"You need space for all the shit you're going to be transporting," Danny informed him of their logic.

"I said a van would be better," Bram added.

"It is a fucking van!" Mark even shocked himself at how emotional he had become over the vehicle they were supplying him with. He told himself it must be the result of all the crank he'd been consuming with Toby for months on end, which made him further think that some time alone on the road may actually be a good thing. These thoughts quickly passed as soon as he popped the hood and saw the engine inside. It took every ounce of strength that he possessed not to attack Danny and Bram. The only way he could calm himself was to see it as a challenge. He'd outrun every piggy in the UK and it could easily be argued that it had been the Dodge Demon he drove and not his skills behind the wheel. This wagon would be a true test of his skills... or   the   death   of   him.

Several of the bikers had taken Toby out of the city and beyond the suburbs until they were surrounded by flat fields and the odd windmill. Occasionally, Toby would have to remind himself that he had done nothing wrong and the club wanted him to continue cooking and churning out cash for them, as the ride felt like something you would experience before being shot in the back of the head and dumped in an unmarked grave. His crank-addled mind caused his eye to twitch and head to jerk at random angles while filling him with an almost uncontrollable urge to leap off the pillion seat at high speed. There had been little said to the cook other than 'get on' before he was sped away on a loud chopper to a remote location where the bikers had a large and abandoned-looking warehouse.

The inside of the place was nothing like the outside. From the road it had looked like a derelict structure just waiting to be torn down, but once Toby stepped through the metal doors he saw a narco chef's Shangri-La. Waiting inside for him were giant vats and long tables full of equipment and utensils, plus all the ingredients he needed – a proper grade A facility for mass producing whatever chemical intoxicants his little junkie heart desired.

Toby skipped merrily up and down the lengths of apparatus, screaming excitedly at all the toys on offer for him to play with. Stood before a far wall of the lab were several men who would be assisting him. They watched the mad chemist making his way up and down the length of the room like a maniac, and looked over to the bikers who had brought him as if to say, 'really? This is the fucking guy?'

Danny motioned for Toby to follow him through another door at the far end of the warehouse. The pair walked into a huge room, flooded with light and filled with runs of containers ready to be used for planting. Toby burst into a hysterical laugh and jumped up and down on the spot.

"Are you… okay?" Danny asked while taking a step away from Toby.

"This is fucking incredible! It's like a dream come true! Mass production of the greatest drugs the world has ever known!"

Toby laughed louder and even more hysterically.

"Well, I'm glad you like it," Danny said while questioning whether or not the club had made the right choice to entrust so much expensive equipment with what was clearly a madman.

Toby suddenly turned and grabbed the slim biker by his arms, "Oh, Danny, Danny, Danny we are going to do magical things in here my friend. We are going to change the fucking world right here in the middle of the Dutch countryside. Mass production of Toby-grade ganja, glass and whatever the fuck else our hearts' desire," Toby released the biker and started to wander up and down the aisles again, singing, "Oh, Danny boy, the bongs, the bongs are calling, from grow to grow and down the—"

"Don't fuck this up!" the biker caught Toby off guard with the sudden change in his mood. "We spent a lot of fucking money on this gear and we expect big fucking results because of it." And with that he turned and walked away with vice-like knuckles.

"Who are these cunts?" Toby yelled after the VP, while pointing at the other men standing and gawping at their new instructor.

"Your helpers," Danny yelled back over his shoulder as he continued to stomp away. Toby screamed and hooted at the top of his lungs. He'd finally made it to the big time. A giant mass producing lab plus a crew of assistants. He almost came in his pants.

Once Toby had started sorting Mark out with primo ganja again he calmed down about the car he'd been given. His plans on racing around Europe while high on meth to test the mettle of the Dutch police were all forgotten and he was finally settled on simply cruising around in the wagon while puffing on copious amounts of high grade. The fact that so much of the cargo the club had given him to move consisted of guns and grenades also made for good motivation not to drive wildly around the villages and cities.

On one of the earlier runs they'd even given him dynamite to take to some thieves living in The Hague. Mark had hoped it was activists he was delivering to, but they turned out to just be really ancient villains who still did things the old-fashioned way. The really old-fashioned way. That had been one of the longest and sphincter-testing drives of his life. The bikers had been upfront about what he was transporting for them, probably for their own amusement rather than as a warning for the driver. He'd heard stories in the past about how volatile the red sticks could be even when not lit, and of course the bikers pumped his head full of tales about crims they'd known in the past who were no longer around because they'd been driving around with dynamite in their bike's saddle bags. Every spliff Mark lit he squeezed out a little more of the tension that was constantly brewing in his stomach.

As the weeks and months rolled on, Mark and Toby saw less and less of each other. The chef was almost constantly at the warehouse producing narcotics while Mark was always out on the road delivering contraband.

When they did meet up with each other things got messy quickly. They were both getting a lot of cash from the Grim Union now due to the insane amounts of money the club were making off their backs and skills. They had spent a little of their wages of sin doing up the flat they shared, but most of it went appropriately enough on whores and booze.

A good night out for the pair usually consisted of dancing and drinking in clubs, followed by driving around with a car full of prostitutes and a head full of acid, weed, speed and whatever else Toby had knocked up recently. Times were good, and the partners decided that they were set to take a chance and ask the Grim Union to help them to fulfil a lifelong dream that they had both   shared.

What had started as a derelict concrete lab with piss-poor supplies had evolved into a full-blown institution with a grow room that could generate hundreds of thousands of Euros a year. Once the Grim Union had moved Toby over to the warehouse out of town he and Mark had slowly started turning the place into a regular-looking flat for living in. Sure, Toby still had a room for growing their private supply of Kryptonite, but the rest of the place was pretty normal now, despite the semi-abandoned neighbourhood. Plush furniture, flat screen TV and even kitchen appliances for making food and not narcotics. Mark and Toby never spent that much time there, but when they did need a place to go to they had it now. The pair wanted something more though.

"You boys are doing good," Vlad said from one of the large cushioned seats. "You are happy with the Union, yes?"

Mark and Toby sat on the couch situated between the chairs that Vlad and his VP Danny sat on. Near the entrance to the room loomed Kong, who in Mark and Toby's opinion would have probably needed the whole couch to himself if he wanted to sit down. To answer Vlad's question, Mark simply nodded an affirmative.

"Things are good, but we want... more." Toby told them what he and his friend were really thinking.

"Really?" asked Danny, surprised considering how much the pair had already acquired.

"We have a dream," Mark said with a touch of melodrama.

"Like the black man, yes? King, yes?" Vlad said with a smile of recognition at the quote.

"This King has a different kind of dream," Mark said returning the smile. "All are welcome, but I want them holding spliffs not hands."

"What?" asked Danny, his faced creased with confusion.

"Picture it boys!" Toby yelled as he leapt to his feet and spread his hands wide before him. "The Atom Café," he said with a smile before imitating the sounds of a crowd cheering their approval.

Kong looked uneasy with Toby's sudden movements, while

Vlad and Danny just looked surprised. Toby stayed on his feet, looking back and forth between the bikers for a little recognition of the sense in his proposal. Instead there was only silence.

"What we're trying to say is that we'd like to have our own coffee shop," Mark brought the bikers up to speed while Toby dropped back down onto the couch having had the wind taken out of his sails.

"Really?" Danny was surprised the pair had thought about going into legitimate business, considering they were degenerate fiends who liked to take as much as they cooked from what he'd seen. When they weren't taking drugs they were fucking hookers. This kind of thinking seemed almost beyond their usual capabilities.

"Is that such a big ask?" Toby couldn't believe the bikers weren't immediately on board with the idea. "Considering how much money we're fucking making you?"

"We give you nice place," Vlad said with a sweeping hand at their surroundings. "Money," he shrugged. "Nice girls," more hand gestures along with raised eyebrows at Mark. "Many girls, yes? Why you want more?"

"Like Mark said, it's our dream. The Atom Café." Again, Toby spread his arms like he was unveiling the Second Coming of Christ rather than another coffee shop in an already overcrowded market. This wasn't far from the truth as he was off his nut on a cocktail of gear and was vaguely hallucinating. Not completely hallucinating, but enough to be able to describe his reality as 'augmented' at the very least.

"We have to think about this," Vlad said with an unconvinced face.

"What's there to think about? We—"

"It's doable," Danny cut Toby off before he went off on one. "We have a lot of legitimate businesses. But opening a new coffee shop takes time, money, connections, legal parameters up the ass..." the biker drifted off and gave another shrug of his shoulders to indicate that nothing was for sure in this situation.

"Is not small thing you ask," Vlad added.

"We're not asking for a new coffee shop to be built," Mark

said.

"We know which one we want," Toby jumped in and talked over his friend with excitement. "We just want to change the name," he couldn't control the exhilaration welling up within him at the prospect of finally having the Amsterdam coffee shop he'd dreamed of for so many years. "And the gear," he added, knowing full well that if he was running a café he'd be supplying it too.

"Which one?" Danny asked before looking over at Kong, their in-club   negotiator.

Bram Jansen had been sticking his fingers in and out of both legitimate and criminal businesses for many decades now, so he knew a thing or two about both worlds. The Grim Union had appointed him club secretary and he had accepted because his past experience suited the position. Perhaps he could have been the club treasurer, but Lucas Visser already had that spot and they were long-term friends and comrades so he wasn't about to step on the man's toes. This is why when he saw the coffee shop situated on the edge of the Red Light district close to De Oude Kerk church he immediately saw the potential it had as a legitimate income and money laundering opportunity for the club. He would never admit it to the two Welsh idiots, but he definitely thought they had chosen well in terms of location for a coffee shop.

The neighbourhood had a giant foot flow passing through from all of the tourists wandering around both De Wallen on one side of the canal and the more genteel neighbouring areas that included things like the central train station into Amsterdam, fancy boutiques and nice restaurants. He smiled and nodded approval as he entered through the narrow wooden door, which was flanked by giant windows that gave a great view of the surrounding area. He peered back over his shoulder out of curiosity as to whether his companion could actually fit through the entrance. Kong had to turn sideways, but he made it in successfully.

As soon as the two bikers entered they casually walked to the counter on the other side of the room, taking in their surroundings that were all decked out in wood. There were several customers sat at the small tables smoking weed and sipping drinks, and a few more on the mezzanine area that looked down on them. There were also several people sat on high stools at the counter, but nobody in the place reacted to the appearance of the bikers, despite one of them being almost twice the size of anyone else in the joint. At the counter the bud tender approached and smiled, "Yes?"

"I'd like to speak to the owner," Bram said returning the smile.

At the far end of the counter a slim man in his fifties turned on his stool to look at Bram and Kong. He was stoned and took a moment to observe them before speaking.

"Welcome. I am the manager," the slim man said slowly. "How may I help you?"

"I have a message for the owner," Bram said sternly. "The Grim Union is going to take over this place. You have two weeks to vacate."

"What?" asked the manager, confused. "But it's not for sale," he said with a shake of his head as he turned back to the counter and waved his hand at Bram as if to dismiss him.

Bram casually lit a cigarette while his colleague began negotiations.

Kong took two giant steps toward the manager of the coffee shop and used his fist to smash the seated man's face into the edge of the wooden counter. The manager's skull could be heard cracking open from outside on the street. His features almost flattened with the force of the blow and then his twitching body dropped down to the grubby floor and started leaking blood onto it. Kong was emotionless as he turned to face the rest of the clientele.

There was a short pause filled with nothing but an unsure silence before all of the customers in the place leapt to their feet and screamed in fear and panic. Everyone ran for the narrow exit and forced their bodies through and out to safety. Kong simply stood and stared at the stoners running past him like they were trying to avoid a grizzly bear or rampaging tiger. Only the bud tender remained where he was behind the counter, his face ashen.

"Tell the owner to come to our bar tonight with the paperwork or my friend will be back tomorrow," Bram instructed the young man as he dropped his cigarette butt on the floor and ground it out with the heel of his boot.

Kong then picked up the stool closest to him and smashed it to pieces on the counter, which was the start of about five minutes of violent destruction of any and everything Kong could get his hands on. The bud tender ducked down behind the counter to avoid the debris that flew through the air, cowering and squealing with the one single thought going through his head: *please*   *let*   *me*   *live*.

"What the fuck happened in here?!" Toby yelled from the centre of the floor. He span around on the spot, tugging at his hair as he took in all the destruction around him. The coffee shop looked like a bomb had gone off in it.

"Kong happened," Danny Ross informed him dryly, standing with the whole Grim Union committee and various other members of the club.

Mark and Toby looked up at the giant biker who stared coldly down at them. There were no real emotions in Kong's eyes or much of anything that could be called human in his countenance. He had that stereotypical serial killer look about him, the kind where if you saw him in a bad TV show you would immediately identify him as the murderer and then spend the rest of the show just waiting for the lead detective to prove what you already knew.

"Did you really have to wreck the place?" Toby condescended.

Kong gave his usual response of a cold hard stare and heavy breathing.

"Does the gorilla not understand English?" Toby asked mockingly.

Before the stupid jib on Toby's face had time to revert to his normal features, Kong had stepped forwards and hoisted him up into the air by his throat. Toby squirmed, choked and kicked frantically as he dangled from the giant fleshy vice-like grip.

"I believe what my partner was trying to say was thank you," Mark said calmly. Even after all the changes he and Toby had been through and the time they'd spent apart, this all seemed completely familiar and expected to him. It was business as usual. Toby says something stupid to someone dangerous, Mark talks them out of killing him. Back to the same-old, same-old. "Nice work. Well done," he smiled at Kong, who then relinquished his grip on Toby's neck, dropping him into a heap on the floor at his big black boots.

Toby could do nothing but lay there gasping for air with water leaking from his eyes and snot running out of his nose. His eyes bulged red and the veins stood out like they were about to

88

explode. Not even their old customer and nemesis Dick, the psychotic gangster and their biggest punter who also happened to be the first victim by way of a stained dildo back in their house on the fateful day that changed their lives, had ever strangled him like that before.

"You are welcome," Vlad van de Berg said with a nod.

"The place is yours to run boys, but make no mistake about it – we still want our crank every week," the VP said to Toby before looking at Mark, "and you'll still need to make deliveries. We'll launder cash through this place, but you still need to make yourselves useful to the club for us to have any interest in you. A legit coffee shop isn't enough to satisfy us." Danny, Vlad and the rest of the Grim Union committee members had already decided that they were going to ride Mark and Toby for all they could get. They would screw every last Euro out of them and then some. "Running a coffee shop just isn't enough profit in itself, yeah?" They were the Union's little cash cow as far as the committee were concerned. They weren't members, they weren't prospects, they weren't even bikers. They were slaves, no more no less.

"Cool," Mark smiled. He knew the score, but wasn't about to let on just how accurately he was reading between the lines. Mark knew how to play without ever showing his hand.

"We'll need to make some adjustments," Toby suddenly croaked as he stood up, hand rubbing his red throat.

"To what?" Bram asked with concern. As far as he was concerned they just needed to refurnish, nothing more.

"Redecorating is at your expense," Lucas Visser said with a wag of the finger. He had no intention of giving the two dope fiends any of the club's money to spend on unnecessary luxuries like flat screen TVs, sound systems, fancy decorations or whatever other bullshit they thought they needed.

"I'm not talking about a new lick of paint boys," Toby said as he started to walk around the coffee shop and explain it to the bikers. "No, no, no. Major renovations need to take place here. I can't be running this place, being a fiend and cooking up at the kitchen you got me in at the arse-end of nowhere." Now it was

Toby's turn to wag his finger. "No sirs. The kitchen needs to be here—"

"Where?" Danny blurted out.

"Grab some shovels and pickaxes boys," Toby said pointing at the floor, "there be digging to be done." Toby had now circled back around and was stood to the side of Kong, who he slapped on the back in a 'let's get to work buddy' kind of way, but ultimately wound up hurting his hand. Kong barely noticed he'd been touched.

"We need to move the grow op and the lab here," Toby continued. "Underground for the kitchen, upstairs for the garden." Toby got back to pacing around as he continued to explain his thoughts to the bikers and Mark. "It's going to be a tough day's work, maybe even a few days, but with some elbow grease and stiff upper lips and perhaps a pneumatic drill or three we'll—"

"You'll," Lucas said unimpressed.

"What?" Toby asked, now frozen mid-step.

"Painting, digging, anything," Lucas replied with a stern finger pointing at Toby. "You do it."

"You wanted this location, we got it for you." Danny brought Toby back to reality. "Any changes you want doing to it are coming out of your pockets and done by your hand."

Toby then strode forwards, pointing at Kong, "But with this beast we could be finished and open again in a matter of—" the moment Toby had walked close enough Kong had him back up off his feet with one giant hand gripped tightly around his throat. "...*days*," Toby managed to squeak through his chokes.

"Make whatever changes you want boys," Danny said sternly while looking back and forth between the silent Mark and dying Toby "But that door doesn't close. Business as usual for the Union from tomorrow onwards. You drive!" a rigid finger at Mark. "You cook out in the sticks!" the finger was now aimed at Toby. "Who operates this place – and when – is between the two of you, but the other shit doesn't so much as stutter in its cash flow."

Mark nodded acknowledgement of the rules laid down by the

bikers. Toby raised a shaky thumb while doing his best to remain conscious.

Vlad smiled.

Kong then dropped Toby for the second time. While he lay in a heap struggling to stay alive, the Grim Union all turned and walked out of the coffee shop. There was nothing more to say. The bikers had made it clear enough that Mark and Toby were nothing more than slaves – possibly employees at best – of the club.

Mark watched the outlaws mount their motorbikes and ride away into the city night, probably chuckling about the fact they now had another legit business to skim cash off as well as the illegal enterprise Mark and Toby were already managing for them.

"How much shit do you want to change exactly?" Mark asked Toby, who had just managed to get back to his feet.

"We need to be able to make the illegal products right here while selling the legal shit," Toby informed him croakily.

"Okay, but—"

"It'll just be some minor foundational modifications, that's all," Toby lied, "and an attic refurb of course," he added.

"The attic shouldn't be much work, but foundation—"

"Trust me," Toby interrupted. He'd chosen this spot not just for the heavy foot-flow location, but also because he had taken the time to study underground blueprints of the entire city. "We also need to think about our Plan B too."

"Our what?"

"You don't really trust those denim dickheads do you?" Toby was shocked his friend could be so naive. "And what about our past, huh?"

"As long as we pay them what they want every month it'll be fine."

"What the fuck happened to you dude?" Toby asked with a hint of pity and disgust.

"What?" Mark was both shocked and offended by the question.

"When did you become the naive twat and I become the savvy

guru?" Toby asked with a disapproving shake of the head.

"This was always the dream dude! A fucking coffee shop in Amsterdam!" Mark spread his arms wide. "We made it a reality, despite everything!" The tone of his voice tried to convey all that they'd been through together. "Don't fuck it up!"

"Plan B," Toby shrugged and pulled a jib as he walked away from Mark. "That's all I'm gonna say. Leave it to me."

Mark hung his head and shook it to clear away the voice telling him that his friend was about to embark on some crazy and foolhardy task that would ultimately wind them both in deep shit or dead.

"Remember, you're the salesman and I'm the cook," Toby said with a nod. "I'll also be taking on the responsibilities of chief architect and foreman for a while," he added with a stern look on his face, "but the coffee shop is yours to run for the time being." Toby was now casually strolling up the wooden steps to the mezzanine area. "You may want to handle any dealings with the queers in leather too. I have a sneaking suspicion that the big one dislikes me."

Mark watched his partner surveying the coffee shop and couldn't help but think that they were repeating history. Only now their house of ill repute had been replaced by a coffee shop and their dangerous and deadly supplier had been replaced by a deadly and dangerous biker gang. Toby was making insane plans while pissing off their task masters, and Mark was being forced to be the one to deal with them and try to keep everyone alive. He was happy they had the coffee shop, but dubious how long it would   last   for.

Chapter 4 – Present

Amsterdam and Diamonds

The sound of a dozen hammers being cocked on pistols at the same time was quite an experience. Not a positive one as far as Mark and Toby were concerned, what with all those guns being pointed at them. The noise was far louder than Toby would have expected it to be if you'd asked beforehand what it might sound like.

"You two are fucking dead men," growled Danny from the semi-circle of leather-clad gunmen facing the dope fiends.

"Vlad, be reasonable," Lucas Visser, the only biker not holding a gun, said to the club president.

"Yeah Vlad, be reasonable," Mark concurred enthusiastically.

Vlad was still sat at his usual place at the main table in the back room of the biker bar. He took his cigar from his mouth to look at his treasurer with a little confusion showing on his rugged face. As far as he was concerned, death by firing squad was pretty reasonable considering how badly the pair had fucked up. Vlad had beaten men to death with his own fists in the past for owing him a fraction of the money Mark and Toby had lost him by blowing up the coffee shop, and then there was the extra heat it brought them from the authorities... well, bullet-riddled bodies tipped into a canal was reasonable in his mind.

"We lost a lot of money, no?" Lucas spoke his mind. "They should have a chance to pay it back first."

"First?" Toby blurted out. The ordinal number made him feel uneasy as it implied more shit to come at a later date despite the imminent threat of death that presently stood before him.

"They're fucking liabilities," Danny growled, his trigger finger tensing.

"Let's just fucking shoot them and be rid of these wank—" Levi tried to back Danny up but was cut short by Lucas.

"They blow up a fucking coffee shop," the treasurer stated in a tone that said he still couldn't believe they'd done it. "This is expensive thing for us." Lucas wagged a finger, as he sometimes did when getting angry about money. "Not just the building, but what we could do with legitimate business." He stared hard at the two fuck-ups. Technically only Toby was the fuck-up, as he'd been the one to blow the place sky-high. And then of course there was the problem with the yet-to-be-identified crispy corpse.

"Fuck all that!" Levi shouted, "They're costing us more than making for us—"

"Lucas is right," Vlad cut the young man off. "They owe us money." He put the cigar back to his lips now that he'd said his piece. To his left, Bram leaned in close and whispered into the club president's cauliflowered ear. Vlad smiled and nodded, almost laughing out loud as he took the cigar back from his scarred and cracked lips. "Yah, this is good idea," he said nodding and smiling at Bram. "Danny, Bram has plan."

Everyone in the room now turned their attention to Bram Jansen, the club secretary.

"J-J. This will happen soon, yes?" Bram slowly looked at each of his fellow bikers. "The boys need more hands, yes?"

"These two fuck-ups?" Danny couldn't believe his ears.

"You can't be serious," seconded Levi.

"You know he can drive," Owen interrupted, pointing his pistol at Mark as an indication of which fuck-up he was referring to. "And you know he's fucking mental," he pointed the gun at Toby. "So..." he pulled a face to indicate that he couldn't see the problem with using the pair for what was being suggested. "Why not these two?"

"Exactly," the president said with an ominous tone and grin aimed at Mark and Toby. "One driver and one donkey."

"Donkey?" Toby openly showed his distaste for this insult.

"You can carry bags, yes?" Bram said rhetorically.

"Hell no," Toby answered seriously. "I don't do manual labour."

"Either you carry or we bury," Vlad said pointing his half-smoked and half-chewed cigar at the cook.

"Carry what?" Mark asked.

"Nothing heavy," Danny answered in a loaded way, but it was short-lived.

"Diamonds," Bram said.

"Like the stones?" Toby asked one of those dumb questions Mark was so used to hearing.

"Yah, as in the expensive jewels people pay lots of money

for," Bram confirmed.

"Doesn't sound too hard," Toby shrugged.

"As in stolen diamonds," Mark brought his partner up to speed. "As in a fucking heist."

"Exactly," smiled Danny.

"I'm a cook, not a thief," Toby reminded them.

"You'll be whatever we fucking tell you to be until you've paid us back, including being a fucking donkey!" Danny snarled with his gun raised again.

Toby stepped forwards toward the pistol, his head held high and skinny chest pushed out.

"Bullsh—"

When they'd said donkey, Toby had taken it metaphorically. Now, squeezed into the back of the van with Kong and two other members of the Grim Union, he saw that they meant it literally. They had done little in the way of briefing him on the plan, but from what he and Mark had gathered before the big day it was meant to be a nat's cunt hair away from being labelled a suicide mission. The bikers hadn't said why, just that it was convenient for them to now have an extra driver and donkey for a heist that was extremely dangerous. At one of the planning sessions (which was basically a piss up where they got all psyched about doing another rip), Toby had heard something about the well-armed security being lax on this particular day and there being a window of opportunity to hit the back room where the diamonds were valued and then temporarily stored.

It almost felt like they were laughing at him, mocking him for the position he was in. Kong certainly was. The big fucker never spoke, but his facial expression screamed amusement at Toby's situation. He sat opposite the cook with a giant grin plastered across his face, his lips curled up into a smile that said he was enjoying seeing Toby in the shit. They could have been on their way to unblock drains the way they were dressed. All four of them were kitted out in black overalls, black nitrile gloves and black boots. Toby was fine with the clothing, it suited the occasion and made him look bad-ass in his mind, but the last part of the get-up was not to his liking.

To Toby's left sat Andras, the Welsh prospect if he remembered correctly. A late twenties guy with a junkie stare. You couldn't see this at the moment though due to the wolf mask that he wore. The wolf had been silent for the entire journey, just staring straight ahead, psyching himself up for the heist. Just like the tiger to Toby's right, silent and staring ahead. Toby wasn't completely sure, but he thought it was the Dutch prospect Stijn under the tiger mask, a very young guy who appeared to be in way over his head just sitting in the same room as the hardcore criminal fraternity, and now here he was in the back of a van on the way to a diamond robbery disguised as a tiger. Toby figured he had been given no choice in the matter, much like himself. He turned his eyes front again and then sighed as Kong gave one more chuckle and placed his own mask on his head. Kong, a man named after an imaginary giant gorilla, now sat and stared at Toby with a fucking gorilla mask on. In Toby's opinion you couldn't really tell the difference between Kong wearing it or not wearing it as he was such an ugly bastard, although Toby did consider that he may be slightly biased about this considering how almost every encounter between the two had included Kong physically assaulting him in one way or another.

Toby let out another sigh before looking down at his own mask again. The lolling tongue and giant floppy ears added to the buffoonish nature of it, and then there was also the eye holes, empty now but seemingly mocking Toby for the position he was in. The cook shook his head with disappointment before putting the donkey mask on his head. He sighed again under the furry disguise and then saw the gorilla chuckling before letting out a godawful donkey noise. "Hee-haw, hee-haw!" screeched the biker, his shoulders jiggling to show his amusement.

"Suck my donkey dick you fucking—" the sound of Kong's shotgun being racked silenced the braying donkey.

Toby looked down at the pistol in his lap. The bikers had given it to him with a smile and a warning to be careful. Why? Because it was empty. The gun was purely for show. A way to intimidate anyone who got in his way at the jewellers, but not actually a real threat unless he hit them with it. Toby looked at the giant sat opposite him, still chuckling, and knew that hitting him with the pistol would probably do more damage to the steel than   the   gorilla.

As soon as the double doors at the rear of the small van opened all four animal thieves leaped out and headed straight for the lavish glass-fronted store. During opening hours it was flooded with light to enhance the beauty and appeal of all the shiny precious metals and rare stones on display in the windows. No sooner had the wolf and tiger pounced they were immediately charging into the store, pump-action shotguns ready to start knocking people down like bowling pins.

The donkey was not so quick on his hooves, but was helped along by the giant gorilla at his rear. Toby briskly stumbled through the glass doors that were situated directly below an engraved gold sign that bore two capital 'J's in slick cursive back to back. In tiny writing that Toby would never have noticed even if he wasn't being rushed into the place were the words 'Jameson Jewels.' Kong followed hot on the donkey's heels, slamming the van doors closed behind him and then closing the store doors once he had passed through them too.

By the time Toby and Kong had entered the customers and staff were already screaming in fright while the wolf and tiger shouted commands into their faces, along with threats of physical violence and possible executions.

The van drove away from the scene quickly and as it went the driver glanced in the wing mirror to check the getaway cars were in place. From one of those cars a face hidden behind a pair of gold Elvis Presley sunglasses engraved with the letters TCB sat and watched with his hands already white-knuckled as they gripped the steering wheel in anticipation of the drive to come.

Mark knew from all that had been alluded to by the bikers over the last few days that this was going to be an all-or-nothing getaway, one of those desperate inner-city police chases that put everyone's lives in danger without any discrimination. He'd spent some time studying a map of the streets and even smoked a little glass and lots of ganja to level his head out, but the car wasn't built for his style of driving and the police were bound to be packing some serious horsepower in whatever they turned up in. Today would be the day he found out if the Dutch police had a driver that could match his skills behind a wheel.

They all knew their positions. Once the four of them had secured everyone inside, Toby was to stay in the front of the store and keep an eye on them plus detain any new arrivals, while the other three went to collect the diamonds. That was the real prize, not the bling up front – just the big rocks out back.

The wolf shoved a middle-aged man in an expensive suit before him as he led the way to the entrance to the viewing and appraising room. The tiger and Kong followed close behind, guns ready to shoot anyone that may come out of the door.

While the three bikers headed for the back Toby decided to use his time in the store wisely and began emptying the displays. He figured that if he and Mark weren't gonna get paid for this, he may as well grab whatever he could.

Outside the door to the rear the three bikers stopped and pressed the suited man against the wall with a shotgun to his head.

"Open up or we'll fucking kill them all!" the wolf barked into a camera lens embedded in the face of the door.

"There's nobody in there," the suit squeaked.

"What?" asked the angry wolf, driving the barrel of the gun harder into the base of the man's skull.

"Don't shoot! I can open it! I'm the manager!" he cried out, shaking in his fine Italian shoes.

Kong stepped forward and shoved the manager against the door. The suited man quickly put his hand on the key pad and entered the access code. After a few moments that felt like an eternity for the manager, the door's mechanism clunked and it slid open slightly to indicate that it was unlocked. The manager went for the door handle but was stopped by an angry gorilla and thrown to the plush carpet beneath their feet. The three thieves charged forwards, guns ready for a shootout, but there was nobody to waste or threaten.

The back room was deserted. Several expensive-looking tables with leather seats were spaced out around the room, but there was nobody sitting on them. Kong and the others didn't waste any time trying to figure out why it was empty and instead set to opening draws and cupboards and anything else they thought may contain the diamonds. They found nothing.

"Where the fuck are the goods?!" the wolf howled.

"They gotta be here somewhere!" roared the tiger.

The gorilla stayed silent. Kong looked down at the manager and noticed that he was sticking his fingers in his ears, like he was expecting to hear a loud noise. *But what loud noise could he be anticipating?* the gorilla wondered. The question he asked himself was answered by way of two hidden panels suddenly springing open in the ceiling at the far end of the room revealing two men with assault rifles. As soon as the hidden shooters opened fire Kong dropped to the floor and found himself eye level with the manager on the carpet. The gorilla stared coldly into the panicked face of the suit.

Behind one of the store counters Toby grabbed another handful of jewel-encrusted bracelets and threw them into the bag he'd taken from a female customer. She'd been reluctant to give up her leather Fendi, but then she didn't know the pistol wasn't loaded. Suddenly, a blast of automatic gunfire rang out causing the cook to duck while emitting a little scream. The donkey cowered behind the counter, peering over the top of it and in the direction of the gunfire once it had stopped. Another volley of shots caused him to duck back down and stay close to the ground until there was silence again. There was now a slight ringing in his ears from the loud explosions of the automatic weapons unloading in the confined space.

"That can't be good," Toby said as he stood up again and stared in the direction of the gun battle. He then looked down at one of the employees laying on the ground, "Nobody's supposed to be back there with machine guns." He said this more to himself than the store employee, who looked neither confused or panicked, just angry. "It's supposed to be their day off..." Toby added.

"This is Jameson Jewels you amateur!" the employee spat at Toby. "Mr Jameson is well prepared for your kind!"

"My kind?" Toby couldn't be mad at the insult, after all it was completely true. He was indeed an amateur thief. This was his first, and hopefully last, time robbing a jewellery store and he most certainly wasn't prepared for it. "I'm just a cook!" he pleaded with the angry employee still lying on his stomach.

"You're a dead man," the employee said slightly muffled by the thick carpet in front of his face.

Another volley of gunfire rang out from the back room, which included two distinct types of gunshot – one an automatic volley and one consisting of single blasts. These went back and forth for a few moments while Toby resumed his cowering behind the counter, and then there was silence and a smell of burning in the air. It was not a smell Toby was familiar with, but obviously it was something on fire. He didn't really care what it was, he'd already made up his mind and announced it to whoever should be within earshot: "I'm fucking done here." He looked down at the open bag he'd been stuffing the sparkly jewellery into and nodded confirmation that it was sufficiently filled and he no longer had any reason to hang around.

As Toby rounded the glass counter and headed for the door he heard groans, shuffles and thuds approaching from the rear of the store. He looked back over his shoulder to see Kong, covered in blood, slowly being pursued by another man also pissing blood and struggling to keep his grip on a large gun. Toby didn't hesitate or second guess his decision to flee. He threw the door open and ran for it to the sound of another shotgun blast.

Mark needed no further prompting. The gunfire could be heard clearly, even from where he was parked further down the street. It was clearly coming from inside the jewellers and obviously shit had gone sideways. He put his foot down and positioned the car directly outside the entrance to the store. In his rear view mirror he could see the other driver gesticulating like he was doing something wrong, but Mark knew better. Gunfire always equalled the need for a quick exit, it was just common sense.

The donkey charged out and ducked down at the sound of the blast, but felt no pain. He skidded to a halt at the sight of the car screeching up in front of him. He didn't check who was driving, just dived in and flattened himself across the back seat. No sooner had he face-planted he felt the vehicle accelerate and heard the sound of rubber doing its best to grip tarmac. That was all the evidence that he needed to confirm that he'd jumped into the right car. When he was finally able to raise his head and check, it was the sight of the gold-rimmed sunglasses that confirmed he'd made the right move.

"What happened?" Mark calmly asked the donkey quivering across the back seat.

"The Grim Union's intel department was slightly, erm, misinformed," Toby said as he removed the donkey mask. "Or uninformed," Toby began to manoeuvre into the front passenger seat as Mark sped up. "Whatever," he said as the car drifted around a corner, "shit went bad." Toby pulled a fat spliff from inside his sock and lit it. "There were people waiting in the back room. With guns." He exhaled. "The biker twats are all dead."

Mark looked at the spliff and then Toby's new handbag and the bulge in his overalls.

"But you got the diamonds?" the driver asked with a look of confusion. How in the hell did Toby manage to a) survive the shootout, and b) get away with the goods? Most perplexing, but not something he wanted to say out loud as he knew it would offend his delusional partner and possibly lose him his half of the spliff.

"I got some bling from the displays in the front," Toby said as he opened both the overalls and the bag, "nothing from the back." He and Mark looked down at the bag of jewellery and then Mark continued to concentrate on the high-speed driving he was doing in the middle of Amsterdam city centre. Locals and tourists dived for safety as the tyres squealed on the cobbles.

"Looks like a decent payday to me," Mark said with a nod and then sudden burst of handbrake movements as he skidded around some oncoming police cars.

"Not for the Grim though," Toby said.

"Fuck the Grim," Mark said dismissively.

"What?"

"They were never gonna let us live dude," Mark spelled it out, figuring that deep down Toby already knew it but wasn't saying as it meant saying goodbye to Amsterdam and the chances of another coffee shop. "I say we take this shit, sell it and start afresh somewhere new."

"How the fuck are we gonna sell stolen bling?" Toby asked. He had no problem with screwing over the bikers and figured Mark was right about them probably intending on killing them any day soon, but he knew nothing about moving stolen jewels.

"We go to Antwerp dude," Mark said with a cocksure smile.

"Antwerp?"

"It's the place to be when it comes to moving diamonds," Mark schooled his friend. "Not sure about the other stuff though."

"How the fuck do you...?" Toby didn't bother to finish the question. Mark had always been full of knowledge that Toby could never marry with the male slag who had a love for drugs that almost matched his own. "Never mind. We got a tail," Toby informed him of the biker still keeping up with them in the second getaway car.

"I know," Mark again spoke with confidence and a knowing that indicated Toby need not worry as he would TCB as always.

The pair shared the spliff and another that Toby had concealed in his boot while Mark drove like a lunatic through the streets of Amsterdam and then out into the suburbs until they made it onto the A10 ring road, at which point the pursuing club member met with a colossal crash involving several police cars. By the time they had made it to the A4, which led them to Rotterdam and not too far from the Dutch border with Belgium, Mark's skills had gotten rid of all pursuers and the pair had finished smoking a fourth spliff.

"Nice," Toby said with a nod and hooded eyes. Neither he or Mark was sure if he meant the driving or the weed.

"Anything you wanna go back for?"

"Nah.   Fuck   that."

The floor-to-ceiling mirrors all around reflected parts, or sometimes all, of the scene on the giant paper-thin television that was attached to one of the walls. No matter which machine he used Mr Jameson was able to observe the videos on a continuous loop.

At the moment he was laying on his bench press. The figure-hugging fabric he wore soaked up his sweat as he heaved the giant plates off their perch via the thick metal bar and slowly lowered it down to his giant chest. Most men his age had given up on trying to have Mr Universe-shaped bodies, but not him. Every day he stepped into his home gym and completed at least an hour of gruelling weight lifting. Cardio was a morning thing; heavy metal was for after the Sun had set. The triple-digit plates were pushed up and lowered again to the sounds of his grunts and growls, and all the while sweat poured from his brow and saliva dripped from his lips. On rare occasions there were people in his life who saw him lifting and said he should go easier, do less, not try to lift like a man of half his age. Mr Jameson's response was usually a mixture of rage and contempt.

His anger was a result of hating anyone thinking they knew better than him and were in a position to try and tell him what to do. He was one of Europe's wealthiest and most powerful men, which was not something you accomplished if you didn't know better than the average Joe. The contempt came from what he considered to be the misfortune of having to listen to yet another loser open their fat lazy mouth in his presence. People who wanted silver slowed down before the finish line. He only knew about the pursuit of gold. And diamonds. He only knew about being the best at everything. Mr Jameson was a business man and therefore he had to have the most money. Mr Jameson was a man and therefore he had to be the strongest. Mr Jameson was the definition of power and therefore he had to punish those who stole from him.

He roared out loud as he finished the set and placed the slightly bending bar back on its perch. He sat up and breathed hard while wiping the sweat from his brow with a towel. He stared hard at the screen showing him the image of one of the thieves that had made it away with a bag of his gems.

The donkey was now broadcast all around the gym in crystal-clear 4k resolution for the bodybuilding businessman to get a good look at and swear silently to himself that he would see the bastard hanging from a rope for having the brass balls to steal gold and diamonds from him.

Mr Jameson was distracted from his thoughts of revenge by the sudden entrance of his secretary, who wore a crisp suit and carried a ringing smartphone in her manicured hand. He took the phone from her without a word and placed it to his sweaty ear to hear it ring once more before being answered.

"Good evening," Mr Jameson said before the other person could give any kind of greeting. "I need you to go to Amsterdam immediately."

"Certainly sir," came the deep reply. "Please send me the details."

Mr Jameson ended the call and passed the phone back to his secretary before laying back down on the bench for his next set.

"Only the two of them sir?" she asked naively.

"They're not like the last pair of hounds," Mr Jameson said with a tone of contempt he always used when his decisions were questioned, even by someone trying to learn from him. "These two are a different breed."

Chapter 5 – Past

Cop Killers Pay the Price

The rear of the prison transport van was cramped and stank of all the abuse it had taken over the years from numerous felons being transported to and from their normal lives. Toby went wild, almost causing serious damage to his own body, rattling the restraints that were attached to his wrists and ankles. He could hardly believe it. First his home had been turned into a morgue filled with 12 dead bodies and he had to take the rap for all of them. Then he got mysteriously released in order to do the further bidding of that malicious cunt TFC by transporting ganja across Wales, and now here he was right back in the clutches of the law – set up for a murder he didn't commit. Two cops no less. Both gunned down by TFC and both deaths pinned on him. At least he had Mark with him this time, even though he didn't seem so positive about that.

"I said I need to fucking piss you sons of discount whores!" Toby yelled at the small panel that remained closed and kept the prison personnel upfront and out of sight.

"Fuck you!" a voice screamed back. The men up front could hear everything that was said in the rear. "Piss in your pants for all we care you cunt!" The guards had no intention of breaking with prison protocol that dictated they stopped for no reason whatsoever. This was the main reason why the van stank as badly as it did. It didn't matter if the prisoner genuinely wanted to piss or shit or whatever or if he was just trying to find a way to escape, like Toby – the van didn't stop until it reached the prison gates.

"Now what?" Toby asked Mark, who still stared out of the tiny window in the rear door.

Mark had no answers. He saw the hopeful face of Paul – a man he only knew as 'The Hitcher' – who had aided them in their last escape from the clutches of the law. He drove behind the prison transport van in a car that had seen better days and smiled up at Mark as if to say *Come on, we can do this*, but Mark knew they were completely fucked. He and Toby were in cuffs and the van wasn't stopping until it reached the prison where a shit-load of armed guards would be waiting to receive them and administer a good old fashioned prison welcome with batons and boots and fists and riot shields.

Mark and Toby had been charged with the double homicides of British police officers, a crime that did not go down well with prison wardens or the guards that served under them. Mark was under no illusions as to the pile of shit he was about to fall in. The prison guards would hurt them – hurt them bad – and keep doing it regularly for killing what they considered to be fellow brothers-in-blue. The fact that they were innocent would mean absolutely nothing to them. The court had found them guilty and sentenced them for the crime, and that was that as far as everyone else was concerned. Mark could feel the depression starting to creep back in under his skin and burrow into his bones. Before Toby had been released and they'd had their wild adventure up and down Wales, he spent the best part of a year in the foetal position crying over his ex-girlfriend Janine and feeling sorry for himself. He felt that blackness seeping into him again, only this time it brought with it a dread of the pain he would endure at the hands of men in uniforms who would punish him while he prayed for death's embrace.

Toby wondered if this prison would have the same delicious meatloaf the last place used to serve up on Thursdays.

Paul could see that the van wasn't stopping and the two nutters locked inside weren't going to be able to do a damn thing about it. This meant that he had to. Extreme action was needed and he had to think of something fast. He decided to stay on the tail of the van until an idea came to him.

By the time the vehicle had reached the prison gates there had only been one option to present itself to the once professional hitcher and former child heir to an empire of extreme wealth. He wasn't a criminal or a professional escape artist. He didn't have weapons or even tools. All he had was a beaten-up old car that he'd stolen. So that's what he had to use.

Paul revved the engine several times and then put his foot down. The lump of metal screeched and screamed as it made better contact with the road beneath its wheels and dragged itself forwards towards its target, which was much bigger and better built. Paul gritted his teeth and then let his jaw spring open as he got closer to the prison van, eventually letting out a war-like scream just before his rusty Peugeot impacted the side of the van sitting stationary outside the prison gates.

Christian and Roger had been driving prisoners around the UK for almost a decade together. Over that time they had become friends as well as good co-workers. Each had met the others' wife and children as well as shared some of their more intimate thoughts and feelings about life and other people. They were both appreciative of the fact that they got on with each other considering how much time they spent cooped up in the small transport vehicle. True, their tastes in music differed but over time a compromise had been met that allowed them to take it in turns to choose what was played on their sometimes lengthy journeys. At no point in all their years together had they run into any major problems. Occasionally you had a prisoner talk some shit to you, but after a swift beating it was back to plain old driving and shooting the shit. Neither man had a problem with beating a prisoner if it gave them a quieter day or easier journey. They were not bullies and had never beaten a prisoner just for the fun of it like some of their colleagues did. All in all, they felt like they were fair and decent hard-working men, just a couple of blue collar Joes not deserving the experience of having a car driven by a lunatic come smashing into the side of them only inches from their destination and last transport of the day.

The Peugeot had reached a fairly decent speed by the time it crashed into the side of the prison van – fast enough for the small car to knock the larger vehicle onto its side. The Peugeot's front end folded up like an accordion and Paul was lucky not to get crushed by the engine block being shunted backwards. The air bag took the brunt of the force, but it burst and let the driver collide with the steering wheel, his arms flailing forwards to punch at the windscreen that shattered spectacularly. Paul was unconscious for a few moments after the smash, but the sounds of alarms and men yelling soon brought him round enough to get moving and start the next improvised phase of the escape plan.

Squinting at the toppled van Paul was relieved to see that the impact of the crash had been sufficient enough to shatter the glass of the vehicle too. He knelt down on the safety glass shards and reached through to retrieve the keys from the unconscious guard. A part of him hoped that they were still alive and wouldn't suffer any long-term injuries, but he knew that thoughts like that had to be pushed aside in order to get the task at hand completed within the minuscule timeframe that remained. He got back to his feet and shakily staggered to the rear doors using the van to support him. The vehicle lay on its side, which had made the reach through the destroyed windscreen to get the keys an easy enough thing to do, but unlocking the rear doors was now proving a challenge to Paul who couldn't get his mind to focus on the slight difference it made when turning the key from this angle. Eventually he managed it and then he got the lower door open to flood the inside with light.

As soon as Paul peered inside he heard, "You fucking lunatic!" yelled at him by a semi-conscious Toby. "I love you!"

"Any more of that kind of talk and I'll leave you here," Paul said nervously.

After fumbling with the keys to their restraints multiple times the trio fell out onto the road and willed themselves to stay conscious and alert. They pushed themselves onto their feet and staggered away from the wreckage.

"I'll drive," Mark announced. He knew the prison guards would be out at any moment to detain them and that the police would arrive soon after.

"Cool," Paul said as he stood and waited for Mark to tell him where to go next.

At this point the three men all realised that they were all stood in the middle of the road, directly outside the prison that two of them were technically escaping from and just looking at each other. Nobody moved, save for Mark's head when it snapped in the direction of the sound of the approaching sirens.

"Where's your wheels dude?" Mark asked Paul, holding his hand out to retrieve the keys to said vehicle.

"There," Paul said looking at what was left of the car he'd used as a battering ram.

"He means the getaway car," Toby realised Paul was not keeping up with Mark's mind.

"Getaway car?" Paul realised neither of them were keeping up with how unplanned and unprepared this escape really was.

"FUCK!" Mark yelled as he caught up with Paul.

"Do you not have a plan?!" Toby screeched.

"I did my plan," Paul answered innocently.

"RUN!" Mark yelled as he turned his back on the looming prison gates and willed his aching legs and body to move as fast they could in the opposite direction just as he heard them begin to crank up the prison sirens.

The trio were fortunate that even when injured the human body can create adrenaline to help it push past any pain threshold it may have to deal with. They were lucky that the guards were mostly overweight, middle-aged men who hadn't done any running in decades. These two fortuitous conditions combined with Mark's Rain Man-like ability to remember street maps and city layouts resulted in the three idiots managing to evade capture by the prison guards, stay out of sight of the police search patrols and eventually hide in a derelict garage.

Hours after night had fallen and the cold had set in, the trio still remained motionless on the bare and dusty concrete floor of the empty garage Mark had led them to. In the far distance the occasional police siren could still be heard, possibly running down another lead on them or maybe just chasing after some other poor wretch on the wrong side of the law.

"Fuck it," Toby said as he stood, stretched and groaned at the ache in his muscles. "If I stay any longer, I'm liable to just turn into one giant pile of shite."

"If we're gonna make a move, now's as good a time as any," Mark chimed in from his back. He'd discovered that lying flat on the dirty cold floor helped to numb the pain of the van crash.

"Move where?" Paul asked from the corner of the room. He'd curled up in the shadows and slept while he could, despite being aware of the dangers of sleeping with a possible concussion.

"Somewhere with a fucking carpet or cushioned chairs would be nice," Toby groaned as he stamped his feet in the hopes of restoring circulation.

"Maybe we'll get you a foot rub while we're at it," Mark mocked as he stood.

"Getting out of the city will be impossible for a while," Paul said, unsure if it was his common sense or fear speaking.

"We just need somewhere close and empty to hole up in," Mark thought out loud. "Then we can think about travelling further afield."

"Any ideas?" Toby asked.

Mark answered with a smile.

Less than an hour later the trio were hobbling along a deserted suburb street. They had decided to space themselves out as the police would be looking for a group of three, but made sure to stay close enough that if anything went wrong they'd all know about it. Eventually Mark stopped outside a semi-detached house and waited for Toby and Paul to join him. He smiled and gestured at the 'For Sale' sign outside the building. Mark then pointed at the empty driveway. Toby and Paul took a moment to look around and see that all the other homes in the immediate area had cars parked outside, and most had another car parked on the street. Toby nodded approval to his partner-in-crime. The three strolled around the house, checking the windows and letterbox for any signs of life within. Once they were all confident the house was deserted they circled around to the rear where Mark found a rock on the ground that he picked up and readied to break the glass in the back door with. Toby stepped in his way with a disapproving look and a wag of a finger. Mark looked confused and then proceeded to watch his friend dig a paper clip out of his pocket and then straighten it. Toby raised his eyebrows with a smile before turning and picking the lock. Within seconds the door was open for them to enter.

Toby swaggered forth, followed by Paul who was eager to get out of sight of any nosy neighbours that might have spied them from an unlit bedroom window. Mark couldn't move. He had known Toby for years and had seen the gigantic change in his friend after his time in prison, but for some reason that one act of being able to pick a lock with a straightened paper clip seemed to blow Mark's mind at just how much Toby had gone from a know-it-all hermit who had an obsession for chemistry and drugs to a fully-fledged con able to escape from locks and go on the run from the law like it was all in a day's work. Two years ago the Toby he'd known would have been having full-blown panic attacks every step of the way on this adventure they found themselves on. Two years ago Toby would have likely gotten them caught by freaking out and drawing too much attention to them. Now, he casually crept the empty city streets, picking locks and breaking into people's homes. This then begged the question in Mark's mind about how much he too had changed over the years. He shook the thought off and followed his companions inside the semi-detached house. A house not too unlike the catalyst where all this madness had begun a little over a year ago.

After silently snooping around the property looking for occupants, the three met back up in the barely furnished living room and Paul turned one of the small lamps on.

"Now this is more like it," Toby said with a big smile.

"Let's rest up," Mark said wearily. "Keep the lights off, it's supposed to be empty."

Toby nodded and then turned the lamp off before all three

headed off to different parts of the house to collapse and sleep in warmth   and   relative   comfort.

The following morning Mark, Toby and Paul convened in the living room at separate times. Each looked battered and bruised, but much better after a long sleep and a wash. An ancient TV was on but muted, and they sat in silence for a while watching the news report and reading subtitles about their escape.

"I hate to say it guys," Paul eventually said, "but I think we should split up." He felt guilty for saying it. "Unless there was any CCTV they don't know I'm with you. I reckon I can just get back on the road and disappear."

"What if they did see you?" Toby asked the obvious.

"The news is only showing your faces," Paul stated what they'd all noticed but hadn't said out loud. "It says a third man helped you escape, but nothing more."

"Maybe they're just waiting to get your name before they release your face to the public too," Mark said cautiously.

"Actually," this now brought an important point up for Toby, "what is your name dude?"

"Paul."

"We owe you Paul," Mark said solemnly, "big time."

"Fuck yeah we do," Toby concurred.

"You should stick with us to be safe," Mark advised.

"Safe?!" Paul couldn't believe his ears. His life had been anything but safe since their first encounter at Llewelyn's Pool Hall in Tongwynlais on the outskirts of Cardiff. Granted, a lot of that was his own doing. For reasons he couldn't quite explain – even to himself – he liked the two madmen and felt a connection with them. They were fellow free spirits and he needed that in his life.

"I have a plan," Mark announced to the two outlaws. "Europe."

"Europe?" Toby echoed.

"Mainland Europe," Mark said with a nod. "It's big enough for us to keep moving for as long as we need to." He'd spent a lot of time thinking up possible options while his companions slept and as he saw it this was their best long-term bet, albeit one of the most dangerous in the short term. "We can even go as far as Asia if we must."

"What the fuck are we gonna do in Europe?" Toby blurted out.

"Avoid TFC for a start," Mark had thought about all the angles of their predicament.

"I forgot about that twat," Toby hadn't really thought about anything except sleep and weed.

"You best believe he's not forgotten about us. In fact, I'm pretty sure we're at the top of his to-do list right now."

"Who or what is TFC?" asked a lost Paul.

"The French Connection," Toby said with a sour look on his face.

"Our old supplier and unofficial boss," Mark filled their third man in on some more background details.

"The cunt that had us arrested and sentenced to however long he felt like putting us in cages for," Toby added.

"Who is he?"

"We think he's British Black Ops," Mark said gravely, "some kind of secret arm of the military that flogs drugs to fund international conflicts."

"Holy shit!" Paul was naive to such things.

"You think he won't find us in Europe?" Toby asked Mark, still doubting his friend's plan.

"He wouldn't expect us to run that far," Mark really had thought this through as much as he could. "He thinks we're too dumb to leave the UK." He knew what little respect TFC had for them now.

"How are you going to get across the water with the police hunting you," Paul got up and started to pace with the fear of being dragged into what appeared on the surface as nothing more than complete madness. "The military are looking for you and all the while having your faces plastered on the news as Britain's Most Wanted?" His head span with the fear of trying to attempt such a logistical cluster fuck. He questioned his own intelligence and sanity for ever thinking that setting the two lunatics free was a good idea and some kind of leveller on the cosmic scales of justice. He'd killed the two men who his father had sent to capture him and then saved two souls as karmic balancing. He now had serious doubts about his own logic or possible lack thereof.

"What do the Brits and their government want least of all during this current political climate?" Mark asked in that smug way that said he was the only one in the room who knew the answer to the question, which meant he was smarter than everyone else. Toby knew that tone all too well as the cook had been using it for most of his adult life too.

"Brains?" was the only real answer Toby could think of. He'd seen very little evidence of their use in recent months.

"Immigrants," Mark corrected his friend. "Illegal ones," he added.

"But we're all British," Paul stated the obvious.

"Got any papers to prove that?" Mark asked, again with a hint of smugness.

"What?" Toby couldn't quite put the pieces together yet as to what his friend was suggesting they attempt.

"This will take balls," Mark stood and sounded like a military general pep talking his troops before a foolhardy battle, "big hairy ones," he gestured next to his own rather large testicles, "...and really shit accents." He gesticulated with a finger at his mouth.

"You're insane!" Paul yelled as he waved his arms frantically in the air.

"Tans and beards would help, but then we have neither the weather nor the time for any of that." He chose to ignore the fact that Toby was already sporting a pretty impressive beard, although he was extremely pale of complexion. "So, French accents and some gibberish will just have to do."

"This sounds like the kind of shit plan I'd come up with," Toby shook his head in disbelief of how far things had deteriorated that he was now the more sensible of the pair. A pitiful time indeed he thought.

"It's insane! You're insane!" Paul screeched at volume.

"I love it!" Toby suddenly leapt to his feet with a smile and nod. Mark and he were finally thinking on the same page. Things hadn't deteriorated, they had evolved. It wasn't devolution, it was expansion and unification, a melding of their minds into one complete and fully functioning entity with a common cause.

"You're both bloody mad!" Paul almost tore his hair out at the thought of being the only sane one of the three.

"Can we wear disguises?" Toby asked excitedly. This answer would be the final proof in his mind that after all these years he and Mark had finally bonded on a higher dimensional level.

"If you like," Mark said uncaring and figuring that it really wouldn't make that much of a difference what crap they wore if they couldn't alter their faces.

"Am I the only sane one here?!" Paul felt like he was talking to himself and growing ever more mad because of it.

"Syrians are pale," Toby said with heightened excitement. "We could probably pass for ISIS!" He smiled widely.

"Nice idea but we want to avoid going back behind bars," Mark said in a calm and soothing tone. He appreciated Toby's enthusiasm for the plan and didn't want to piss on his chips, but one of them had to try and keep this plan relatively sensible in order for it to work.

"You're right, Muzzas are too dangerous right now." Toby saw Mark's logic and again took it as evidence of a strong bond between the pair. "Frogs it is!"

"Can you not fucking hear yourselves?!"

"It's the only way," Mark shrugged at Paul.

"We'd stand a better chance of fucking swimming to mainland Europe!"

"Be cool," Mark made calming motions with his hands in Paul's direction and spoke in a hushed tone. "We go to the nearest Immigration Reporting Centre. We explain in French and a little broken English that we don't have any papers or money, then—"

"Then Robert's your father's brother with garlic breath and a permanent red wine stain on his double chin!"

"What?!" Paul screamed.

"They'll ship us over the channel and hand us over to the French filth—" Mark explained further details, but hit a sore spot with Toby.

"Hang on—"

"We then have it away on our toes first chance we get—"

"It'll never work," Paul tried to interrupt the two crazies.

"Walk straight into the hands of the French fuzz?" Toby pulled a sour face as he asked the question.

"Once we're across the water, we've got all of the European mainland to run and hide in," Mark explained the logic to his plan "an entire fucking continent! Plenty of places to keep a low profile!"

Silence filled the air while Toby digested the idea and Paul tried to figure out even more logical arguments against such a foolish dive into the mouth of madness and hands of the authorities they had just escaped from.

"I know it's a shit plan," Mark conceded. "I know this," he nodded solemnly. "But I don't really see any other options presenting themselves to us right now."

"We can just lay low here in the UK," Paul pleaded. "It's only a matter of time before the news stops showing your faces and people start to forget about—"

"The French Connection will never forget," Toby stated ominously.

"Exactly," Mark said wide-eyed and impressed with how Toby was thinking straight about this whole shit storm they found themselves in.

"The cunt won't stop until he finds us and either bangs us up or buries us," Toby said to Paul.

"I dropped off the grid easy enough here," Paul continued to argue against the plan. "We just keep our heads down."

"He's got access to every camera, smartphone and fuck-knows-what-else in the UK," Mark explained the reality of their situation to Paul. "He'll find us eventually, it's just a matter of time."

"At least in Europe we'd stand a chance of staying hid," Toby explained. "It's a tiny chance, but still…" Toby pulled a face that said, 'fuck it, it's all we got.'

"But it's nuts!"

"We have to try dude," Mark said calmly. "Our only hope

right now is that the British authorities are more racist than competent."

"Shit dude," Toby said looking astonished, "you almost make it sound easy when you put it like that."

The journey into Cardiff city centre and to the Immigration Reporting Centre had been a slow one in order to ensure nobody got spotted. As before, the trio had travelled within a distance that they could see each other but not look like they were together. Each had donned hats, sunglasses and scarves that they had stolen from a charity shop. They knew that they needed to cover up without it being obvious that they were covering up.

Once inside the centre they spoke briefly at a receptionist in broken French until eventually a middle-aged fat man signalled for them to follow him into his office. The English receptionist did speak other languages, but she didn't speak French.

The immigration officer's office was cramped with all four of them inside and there were only three chairs, one of which was occupied by the officer that slumped on the opposite side of his very old and beaten-up desk. His computer was off to one side and the keyboard rested directly in front of it so that he could look directly at the trio of so-called immigrants and then away to the computer screen out of their sight as and when he needed. Mark and Toby occupied the chairs while Paul stood nervously near the door. He figured he should be furthest away from the officer as he couldn't speak any French and was absolutely petrified of their half-arsed plan. As far as he was concerned, being near the door made it easier for him to run when it all went to shit.

"So none of you speak English, right?" the officer asked, already sounding fed up before he'd even met them properly. This was the typical British office worker attitude when having to deal with members of the public, particularly the public that didn't speak English and you knew were about to cause you headaches.

"Un petit poi," Mark said in a shit French accent after making the sign for 'a little' with his finger and thumb.

Both Mark and Toby nodded confirmation of what Mark had said.

"And none of you have the required legal documentation to be here in the UK either if I'm understanding this correctly?"

The trio stared blankly.

"Little English," Toby announced in a Parisian accent. Again, Mark gave the man the finger and thumb gesture.

"Right," said the officer. He'd already had a long enough day deporting Muslims without adding some stupid French illegals into the mix. He lifted the receiver on the old phone on his desk and dialled an internal extension number. "Yeah, I'm gonna need a translator," he said into the phone before listening to the person on the other end. "French," he grunted several times. "Cheers." He hung up the phone and then smiled a big fake smile at the trio of idiots.

"Problem?" Mark asked, in what barely passed as a French accent.

It was now the Immigration Officer's turn to use his finger and thumb to make the signal for 'little.' For the next 10 minutes or so the four all sat in complete silence. Mark, Toby and Paul stayed mute for fear of slipping up and giving away the fact that they weren't French. The Immigration Officer stayed silent simply because he didn't like talking to foreigners. The reason he put up with the shit he had to in his job was because he wanted to get as many non-Brits off of UK soil as he could. He was a British bulldog through and through. Anyone who wasn't should get off his island as far as he was concerned. He was a Farage fan and the EU could go fuck itself.

Eventually the silence was broken by a slight knock on the door before it opened to reveal a young man in casual clothes. He entered and nodded 'hello' at the Immigration Officer.

"Three frogs," the officer said dryly. "No English—" he stopped himself before looking at Mark. "Sorry, a little English." He flashed another shit-eating smile.

The translator looked down at Mark and Toby as Paul had looked at nothing but the worn-out carpet for the last quarter of an hour. "Hello," he said with perfect French pronunciation even though he was English. "Can I see your documents, please?" He spoke fluently like a native.

Mark forced himself to remain cool behind his sunglasses. He hadn't expected the centre to have a fluent French-speaking translator on hand. He knew that this cunt would see right through his crap accent and Renault Clio lingo.

"We're sorry, but we don't have any of the correct legal documentation to be here in the UK," Toby suddenly said in perfect French. Even a true Parisian, born and raised under the Eiffel Tower, wouldn't have known he was faking it. "We smuggled ourselves into the country illegally via a shipping container several months ago, but have been unable to get any work or money to survive," Toby continued without hesitation, stuttering or flaws. "We would like to return to France where we can at least speak the language and not worry about the authorities arresting us for being in the country without the appropriate documentation. We apologise for the inconvenience this causes, but we decided to take the gamble due to the scarcity of jobs back home—"

The bewildered translator held up a palm to silence Toby.

"Ship 'em back across the water," the translator said to the Immigration Officer, already worn out by Toby's ramble. "Let the frogs deal with them." Then the young man turned and walked out of the office.

Mark and Toby looked at the officer wide-eyed like they had no idea what was going on, while Paul continued to stare at his feet. The officer gave another fake smile and then began typing up the required files on his computer.

Silence filled the air as hope filled the trio of outlaw's hearts.

The bus was small and old, much like the man who drove it. The Immigration Centre and British government saw no reason in expending man power or budgets to transport immigrants, illegal or not, back to the mainland if they were going of their own free will. As far as the authorities were concerned one old man with a large enough vehicle for the number of bodies was all they needed.

The driver had done the journey countless times now and had never had any trouble. For him it was a by-the-numbers kind of an affair, so he kept his hands on the wheel and his eyes on the road. The journey from the Immigration Centre to Port of Dover wasn't long enough to warrant any stops, which meant there were no hassles for him. It was just one straight drive to the port, cruise onto the fairy, have a drink at the bar and then deliver the cargo to a centre in Calais. Today's trip consisted of the usual handful of Arabs and a few Europeans. No Africans this time, which the driver was thankful for as they were the ones who made the most noise. The Muslims and mainlanders tended to just sleep or keep quiet.

At the back of the bus, Mark, Toby and Paul sat in silence. Mark and Toby had smirks on their faces, but Paul still looked just as terrified now as he did when Mark had first suggested the plan. As far as Mark and Toby were concerned, they were free and clear. Customs should be no problem as they were illegal immigrants with no papers to check after all.

At Dover the bus barely came to a stop at any of the checkpoints. The driver knew most of the staff and officials by first name and those who he didn't seemed just interested in his paperwork and nothing more. There were no thorough checks of the bus, no pat downs or questions. Mark, Toby, Paul and the other several illegal immigrants just sat and waited in their seats.

Mark chuckled to himself at the ease of being able to get out of the country for anyone the government knew to be a foreigner, and then looked at the other people on the bus and figured they had had a far more difficult time getting in than they were having leaving.

Toby cursed himself for not getting some weed for the

journey. Everything happened so fast and so publicly that even he had decided that scoring was too big a risk.

Paul questioned why the hell he had ever helped the two lunatics in the first place. They seemed to be forever dragging him into ever more crazier flights from the authorities.

On the journey to Dover the driver hadn't bothered to check if anyone needed a break or refreshments. Once they were on the ferry he had immediately gone to take care of himself leaving the illegals locked inside the bus. Most of the immigrants were asleep anyway, which the trio of outlaws were happy about.

"Almost there boys," Mark said with a grin.

"I still can't believe it worked," Paul said nervously.

"Never underestimate the racism of British authorities dude," Mark grinned wider.

"Are we really going to just wait here for the French government to take us in?" Toby suddenly asked, not really understanding that part of the plan.

"I don't see how else we'll get through customs," Mark answered.

"Won't they check who we are?" Paul was visibly shaking at the thought.

"How?" Mark asked in a tone that screamed he felt Paul and his question were stupid. "We don't have any IDs."

"They could have scanners for our fingerprints," Toby thought out loud. "That could give them instant access to who we are. Or at the very least show that we're not actually French citizens."

"Shit," Mark said, having not thought about the authorities and their use of modern technology.

"Why didn't they do that back in the UK though?" Paul asked.

"Too expensive or maybe they just want to get rid of us non-Brits," Toby voiced his thoughts again.

"We need to get off this fucking bus," Paul squealed.

"Do we?" Mark asked rhetorically.

"Yes!" Paul leapt at the rear doors and rattled them to no avail.

"Think about it," Mark smiled. "We slid through Dover like a curry through a nun. Who's to say we won't do the same at Calais?"

"I'm fucking done with you lunatics and your stupid plans!" Paul continued to frantically try and budge the locked doors. "I was happy and off the grid until I got kidnapped by you!"

"You saved us you twat!" Toby spat back.

"I know! I'm an idiot!" Paul screeched as he dropped to his knees in defeat.

"Sit back and relax dude. You can't do anything now, we're out at sea," Mark said soothingly as he reclined as much as he could.

"Lifeboats!" Paul exclaimed as he got back up on his feet and began ramming his bony shoulder into the doors. "I can steal a dingy and row to freedom!"

"Good luck with that man," Toby said as he too slid down and back onto the seat.

Paul continued to screech and swear at the locked doors for a little while longer and then finally slumped back into his seat. He was still trapped with the two crazy bastards and heading into the lion's den. He would surely get ID'd and before long his father would be notified and have him collected. Who knows what would happen then?

At Calais, the bus rolled off the ferry and towards the custom's checkpoint. In a small booth that housed the controls to the barrier sat a very fat man in his thirties. He stared slack jawed at his smartphone while smoking a cigarette and eating chocolate. The French customs agent passed his eyes over the driver's paperwork and then stamped it. He barely gave the bus a glance before pressing the button to raise the barrier. They cruised through and at the back of the bus the pair of madmen fought the urge to scream with hysterical laughter at the lack of security.

The other immigrants being transported to France sat in shock, staring wide-eyed and mouths agape as the bus rounded a corner and revealed to them a giant number of people clambering at the outer fence of the port and the impenetrable barbed-wire gates that were locked and separating the port authorities from them.

"Welcome to France dudes," Mark said in shock at the sight of so many people all attacking the outer perimeter of the port.

The driver hit the brakes and stared through the windscreen. It took him a moment to notice the security officer decked out in riot gear knocking on his window.

"What the bloody hell is going on here?" the driver asked the officer once the window had been lowered.

"Same old, same old. Illegal wannabe immigrants and refugees," the officer answered through his visor. "They regularly swarm the fence. Not usually this close to the main gate, but…" he shrugged. It was obviously nothing new and shocking to the officer, but to everyone on the bus it looked like the end of the world or a zombie movie. Wave after wave of human bodies charging at the fence and attempting to scale it like their lives depended on it, doing their best to withstand the barbs, razor-wire and electric shocks from the officer's cattle prods.

"Well, what the hell am I supposed to do? In all my years doing this run I've never bloody seen this bull—"

"Use the other gate," the officer said like it was obvious. Calais was a big port and there were obviously other ways to get in and out. "Or wait. They'll give up and go back to their camp in the woods soon I reckon. Just like always."

The driver nodded and did a 180-degree turn back to the checkpoint, where he was vaguely directed to the next set of gates. After a few wrong turns the bus eventually made it to an exit. The driver showed the already stamped paper work and was then free to drive out of the port and get on his way.

The road from the port was narrow and clearly not the exit for tourists, freight and the bulk of travellers. The tarmac led through tall trees and little else until, yet again, the bus driver was forced to slam his foot on the brake. And yet again he was met with the sight of a giant swarm of human bodies charging forwards. Only this time they came from the sides as well and there was no fence between them.

Everyone on the bus started to yell and scream as a wave of bodies smashed into the rickety bus from all sides and then rocked it like they were back out at sea on rough waters.

"What the fuck is this?!" screamed Paul.

Mark and Toby nodded wide-eyed at each other while all around them the windows shattered. They smiled before Toby retrieved his paper clip and then quickly unlocked the rear doors. No sooner had the doors opened the cook was crowd surfing his way to freedom. He looked back to see Mark launching the hysterical Paul out and then diving after him. The trio all landed gracelessly onto the road before standing and watching the bus fill with new people while ejecting the original occupants. The driver still cowered at the front, screaming for his life.

Mark and Toby grabbed Paul and made a run for the tree line and into the shelter of the woods.

"Where exactly are we headed dude?" Toby asked Mark, staring out at the French surroundings and not having any urge to explore them.

With a giant smirk Mark turned and said the words, "All roads lead to—"

"—Amsterdam!" Toby yelled at the top of his voice. He also had a giant grin on his face and was looking like a small spoiled child on Christmas morning.

"Fucking right they do," Mark said with a nod.

"Awesome plan my friend," Toby said while fighting the urge to kiss him.

"Time to set up a real shop."

"A fucking coffee shop! The fucking Atom Café! Ohhh shiiiittt!" Toby hollered as he proceeded to dance a jig right there in the woods.

"Not me," Paul said quietly.

"What?" Mark asked with a sideways glance.

"I still maintain I'm safer alone," Paul felt somewhat bad for saying it, but there was no denying his life had taken a turn for the seriously fucked up ever since he'd met the pair of criminals. "Now all I see are more roads to hitch along," he said pointing at the tarmac running parallel to the woods they strolled through. "It'll be quite the adventure for you two."

"What the fuck man! You bust us out of prison and con your way to Europe with us and then just fuck off on your own little adventure?" Toby shook his head. "Why'd you even hook up with us in the first place?"

"Yeah, dude," Mark joined in. "Why did you break us out of that van?"

"It seemed like the right thing to do at the time."

"The right thing…?" Mark was very confused by this answer. "But we kidnapped you from a pool hall—"

"—we stole your drugs and took you on a police chase across Wales," Toby cut in, believing the gear they took to be the most important part of the story.

"We didn't even know your name until after you'd rescued us from the law *twice*. I'm pretty sure you still don't know our names."

"But you say it seemed like the right thing to do? Are you sure about that?" Toby chimed in again.

"You're free spirits, like me." Paul explained. "I could see that a cage was as wrong for you as it was for me."

"You were locked up?" Mark didn't recall the hitcher ever mentioning that and he certainly didn't look the prison type. Not the surviving prison type anyway, although he had previously thought the same of Toby.

"In a way," Paul continued. "My father is a very powerful man. Living under his roof was the equivalent of being a prisoner."

"Who's your old man?" Toby asked.

"Unless you're the kind of person who considers politicians and royals to be your underlings, you won't know of the all-powerful Mr Jameson."

"He probably has connections to TFC," Toby said with raised eyebrows.

"Possibly," Mark concurred, while recalling a pair of identical dazzling green eyes just like Paul's that he had met not so long ago, as well as a family name that rang a distant bell.

"My father is money, not military," Paul said. "Banking, not black-ops."

"Banking?" Toby echoed.

Paul nodded solemnly.

"The real rulers of the world," Toby continued with a wry smile.

"Exactly," Paul continued nodding.

"Scum of the Earth!" Toby screamed suddenly.

"He doesn't just run banks," Paul explained further. "He's into trading precious metals and diamonds and sugar and anything else that makes obscene amounts of money."

"So you left a life of obscene wealth to hitch across Wales?" Mark asked with a look on his face that said he was having trouble believing this.

"Yep," Paul said suddenly smiling. "Best decision I ever made."

"And you think we're fucking crazy?" Mark said in disbelief.

"Like I said," Paul stopped smiling, "different kind of cell."

"I understand dude," Toby said as he put his hand on Paul's shoulder.

"Well, if you're not coming to Amsterdam where you gonna go?" Mark switched gears.

"I'll go my own way once we're over the border," Paul said.

The trio walked in silence for many miles through the damp woods and the occasional immigrant makeshift campsite. Mark and Paul both had their minds on where to go first and how to survive. Toby dreamed of The Atom Café.

Mark walked through the service station car park confidently and casually. He'd left Toby and Paul back in the woods while he looked for suitable wheels to jack. The concrete was slick and shiny from earlier rainfall that now reflected the lights from the overhead lights and the few vehicles that were still moving around. All in all the car park was quiet with a decent number of vehicles for him to choose from.

He spotted a little Golf GTI that wouldn't have been his first choice under normal circumstances but tonight it would do just fine. It didn't stand out, it didn't have a particularly difficult engine to hot wire and was nimble enough to come in handy should they get into any trouble. Mark checked there was nobody close by and then smashed the rear passenger window with a stone before opening the door and climbing in to get the engine started.

As he fiddled with the wires one of the signs on the roof of the main service station building caught his attention. It was for some new sandwich one of the crap cafés inside were selling and it was all in French so he couldn't understand it, but it was enough to make his mind wander and allow old memories to creep up on him. Memories he hoped were long buried, much like   the   person   who   occupied   them.

The restaurant was high class and was located down a discreet corner of one of London's less touristy spots. It had an air of exclusivity about it and had obviously been placed in a location where you could find it if you were specifically looking for it, but wouldn't happen upon it by accident while out looking for a quick burger.

Janine had been badgering Mark for weeks now to take her to this place in order for her to indulge in the exquisite French cuisine served up by master chefs now living in London from the continent. Mark couldn't have cared less. They may as well have been going through a McDonald's drive through for all he cared. The only thing that mattered was that eating here would shut his girlfriend up until she found some other shit to harass him about. He hadn't minded the drive from south Wales to the UK's capital, it was only a high-speed three-hour trip down the M4 while smoking weed and snorting cocaine, just a normal evening spin really. He didn't mind knowing that he would be paying extortionate prices for tiny potions of food. He could tolerate the snobs giving him sideways glances between mouthfuls of food and wine. What he had difficulty with was having to wear formal attire.

Mark was a casual guy most comfortable in denim and not with a tie wrapped around his throat. Janine had insisted that he 'make an effort' and wear a shirt and tie. The shirt was no big deal, but he'd never understood how wrapping a silk noose around your neck made you look smarter or more civilised. In Mark's opinion it just made you look like a cunt or a lynching begging to happen. Still, he couldn't deny Janine looked amazing. Sure, she was hot any old time of the day or night to his eyes, but dolled up to the nines to dine at one of the most expensive restaurants in the UK, she looked like she should be served up on a plate for the house special desert. Mark licked his lips and drank in the sight of the woman he adored.

"What do you think?" Janine purred. She was extremely happy. Not only had he brought her as promised, but he'd also got them a fucking window seat. She was so impressed with him she wouldn't have objected to him throwing her over the table and ravaging her right then and there in front of everyone. He certainly looked like he was thinking the same thing the way he stared across the table at her.

"It's all right," Mark answered honestly, which wasn't always the best thing to do with Janine.

"*All right?*" The mood changed. "It's the best fucking restaurant in the city. No, fuck that, the best restaurant in the country."

"The steak was tiny babe—"

"Tiny?!" She almost shat in her Victoria's Secrets the rage bubbled up and over so quickly. "Mark, it's not about the size, it's about—"

"You didn't say that the night we met," he said with a filthy grin.

Janine rolled her eyes and smiled. He was a degenerate and had little in the way of class, but he had plenty of other damn fine qualities.

"It's about the flavours," the words oozed from her lips. "It's about the presentation," she sat up and gently pressed her generous chest forwards. "It's about the ambience," she gestured with one delicate hand at their surroundings. "It's—"

"It's over priced and under sized Janine," Mark spoke bluntly. "Doesn't matter how much you arse it up, it's still just—"

"You have to be one of the least cultured men I have ever met Mark Anthony King!"

"Not the tiniest though, hey?" He smiled and jiggled his eyebrows like something from a Carry On movie.

"How many countries have you been to?"

"Two."

"Which ones?" she asked with a tone of surprise. She could have sworn he'd never left the UK.

"Wales and England," Mark answered without a hint of sarcasm.

"You're *from* bloody Wales Mark," Janine said defeated. "We're in England now, just to go to a fucking restaurant."

"You wanted to come here babe," Mark said before sipping some more wine that he didn't really care for.

"I know I'm the one who—" Janine stopped herself and calmed her nerves with some deep breaths. "Look, my point is you need to expand your horizons and grow a little as a person." She tried to sound nurturing, not annoyed. "You're a smart guy with a lot of potential, but you're just wasting your life sat at home flogging gear to fuck-ups all day every day."

"And I make a lot of money doing it," Mark said sternly. "Toby and I are minted in case you haven't noticed."

"It's not about—"

"You see anyone else as young as us eating here?" he asked rhetorically. When they'd first arrived the pair had spent some time giggling about how everyone else in the restaurant was at least twice as old as them. "I wouldn't be surprised if I'm one of the richest people in this fucking joint, and I'm still in my twenties."

"It's not about money Mark," she growled slightly with frustration.

"Then what are you getting at?"

"Growth and personal development," she spat. "Seeing the world. Experiencing life. Surely you don't want to spend the rest of your days selling dope and getting mashed with Toby, do you?" She hoped he wouldn't just answer yes to the question but couldn't be sure.

"Babe," he leaned forwards with sincerity "I got enough cash to drive us several hours to the most expensive restaurant in the UK without breaking a sweat. I got the kind of spare change that could buy this place and still have a large enough roll left in my pocket to choke the horse they served us. I got that money selling gear with Toby. And sure, we probably take more than we punt out to people, but when you're making as much profit as us what does it matter?"

"It matters because you're getting older and not evolving," she came right back at him with the answer.

Mark slumped back confused and frustrated. "Help me out here Janine," he almost pleaded to her. "I'm lost," he rubbed his weary and dry eyes. "What are you saying to me?"

"For fuck's sake Mark," she hissed under her breath. "I'm

saying I want to start a proper life with you." She stopped to take a breath and calm herself. If she was going to do this then she should be positive and not pissed off. "I'm saying that in order for that to happen you need to be doing more than sitting on the couch playing video games and supplying whatever to junkies."

"You want me to quit dealing?" He spat the wine back into his glass and a little over himself.

"Things are going well for me at the bank babe," she smiled. "They've offered me a promotion," she smiled more and meant it. "They have a branch in Paris and they'd like me to—"

"Paris!" he almost leapt up out of the plush leather seat. "As in fucking Paris in fucking France?!" he bellowed.

"Keep your voice down," she said in a hushed tone while trying to ignore almost everyone in the restaurant staring at them. "Yes, 'fucking' France." She pushed the urge to hit him down deep. "How many other places called Paris do you know of?!"

"So that's why we had to drive all the way to London to eat in this restaurant," he nodded in understanding of her grand scheme. "You wanted to give me a taste of France, is that it?" He shook his head in disbelief at the lengths she'd gone to on this one.

"Yes!" she conceded angrily "Well, that and I'm sick of the crap restaurants we usually go to."

Mark started to say something back at her, but then realised her last statement was one he agreed with. The restaurants around their way were indeed pretty crap.

"Just think about it, okay?" She smiled again. "I'm not asking for a decision immediately, but I do have to let my bosses know if I'm interested or not. And yes I am interested Mark, but I'd like you to be there with me." She leaned forwards and extended her hands across the table towards him with a warm smile. "This could be good for us."

"What the fuck am I going to do in France?" He could not have been less enthusiastic about the idea. "I don't even like wine." He held the almost empty glass of Pouilly-Fumé up for Janine to see more clearly.

"Jesus Mark," she almost slumped face first onto the ornately decorated table covered in fine white linen.

"I got a lot going on in Wales Janine," he pictured how both Toby and The French Connection would react to him announcing a sudden departure to the continent. "You don't realise just how big me and Toby are." He pictured the insane amount of money they had lining the walls, under the floor and in the ceilings of the house without all they had buried when off their nuts at random spots around the Welsh countryside. "How much gear we really sell. Who we—" he had to stop himself before he mentioned he-who-must-not-be-named for fear of an acid bath.

"Look, all I'm asking is that you give it some thought." She forced herself to be more positive and perky. "I love you Mark and I want to be with you."

"I love you too, but France is a big change Janine," as well as being a country he had no interest in. "I've never so much as done a week in Ibiza and now you're talking about emigrating."

Janine stared into his eyes and saw into his heart. She knew better than anyone what he desired most and what made him tick.

"Let's start with something a little easier," she purred with a smile. "It's our anniversary soon." She leaned forwards again, presenting him with a fine view of her décolletage, and spoke softly. "Why don't we go somewhere for a romantic weekend together?"

"Where?" Mark knew that if the word 'France' came out of her mouth he'd lose the plot.

"Scotland has some beautiful areas," Janine knew better than to suggest somewhere that required a passport or where the population spoke a foreign language. She had to break him in gently to the idea.

"It may as well be France for all the good it'll do me trying to understand their accents, that's for sure."

"Try and be positive babe," she tried not to sigh or be cynical. "You won't regret it, I promise." She smiled seductively. She knew him well and understood what he wanted most in life. Janine raised up from the chair and leaned halfway across the table. Mark met her there and they kissed passionately. She knew how to push his buttons, and as far as he was concerned she could press his main one right there and then. When the kiss ended his smile told her she was on the right track to getting what she wanted.

The wires sparked and the engine turned over. Mark gave the gas pedal a few nudges with his foot to make sure she was purring right and then cleaned the wires up and pushed them back into the broken housing he'd ripped them from.

He shifted awkwardly in his seat trying to push the old memories of Janine and Scotland back down into that black box he kept his past horrors locked away in. Still, today – even after all this time – he couldn't think of or hear the word 'Scotland' and not get a burning sensation around his arsehole. He took a breath and then shifted the car into first. *Time to grab the others,* he told himself while locking the black box up again.

They'd offered The French Connection another office, one with a window that he could open. He had refused it, believing instead that the cramped and windowless room suited his feelings about his current posting better. A posting that would more than likely last until he retired, KIA now being off the table due to him being for all intents and purposes a desk jockey. Deep down he figured this was also why he chain smoked so much in the box he worked out of. If a bullet wasn't going to end the monotony for him then maybe aggressive and inoperable lung cancer would do the job. His smoking was the reason the department had tried to give him an office with a window he could open. They weren't trying to be nice and reward him with a picturesque view and fresh air, they were trying to prevent him stinking the entire section out with his insistence on chain smoking in his office. Regardless of how many times he had been told or the number of official warnings he'd received, his response was always along the lines of 'go fuck yourself' before he lit another cancer stick and blew carcinogens into the face of whatever prick was telling him he couldn't smoke in the building. He knew full well they couldn't fire him. Men in his line of work either died or retired – those were the options.

The coffee was strong and black and it went well with the smoke and his general mood. As a field agent he'd been alive and full of vigour. As an in-house operations officer he was essentially dead already. Sure, he had to go out on occasion, but that just meant going out to somewhere in the city or some other part of the UK that was just as safe and boring and bland. After decades of ducking enemy fire in the harshest of climates in the most baron of landscapes, a desk job in the city was torture. Others in his position welcomed the quiet easy life but for him it was hell on Earth. Action, and the accompanying adrenaline rush, were all he'd known for years. The military had trained him to survive anywhere, kill anyone, endure anything, but not this – not a desk job and a fucking tie.

The French Connection was ripped from his thoughts by the sound of his office phone ringing. He sighed a lungful of smoke out as he picked up the receiver, "Yes?"

"Sir, there's a problem," said another man's soft voice. "The DO would like to see you in the Surv. Immediately, sir."

The call ended so he placed the receiver down and grabbed his lighter and packet of Marlboro he was currently working his way through. The Director of Operations was called Terry Rickles and he wanted to see him in the Surveillance Room. It didn't take a genius to figure out that this had something to do with his former pet Mark and his fuckwit partner Toby. They were scheduled to arrive at the prison over an hour ago. Maybe Mark really hadn't been able to handle the reality of living in a cage and done something stupid and violent enough to get himself killed. Or maybe he had even killed himself...

The stroll to the Surveillance Room had taken him past several other people working in the building, and none of them had been happy about the fact he was not only smoking in his office but in the corridors and lift as well. One of them even told him to put it out, but he hadn't really been paying attention. He'd been lost in his thoughts about Mark and Toby and all the shit they'd put him through over the last year or so. Mark had shown promise from the start in the same way Toby had shown contempt from the beginning. They had been his biggest earners until that fateful day when 12 people had died in their base of operations, or drug den depending on the parlance you used.

Inside the Surveillance Room he knew that smoking would not be tolerated and the headache wasn't worth lighting up. He entered and stood behind several operators who were all busy tapping away on keyboards and talking through headsets to various other departments, but his focus was immediately taken by the main monitor on the far wall. The huge screen was flanked by smaller screens showing alternative angles of the same scene. He felt his jaw clench and his teeth start to grind against each other at the sight of the videos being played for the whole room to see. The operators were busy, they had already watched the footage and were now into the next phase of the operation – retrieving more footage.

The large flat screen showed an almost bird's eye view of Mark, Toby and another young man running from the toppled prison van. The camera appeared to be situated on a high wall just in front of where the van lay on its side. He deducted that it must be one of the cameras placed along the giant perimeter prison wall, and then noticed that the other screens were showing footage from similar heights but at different angles. This told him that the van had been attacked right outside the gate by the third man. He racked his brains for a likely candidate but couldn't think of anyone left alive in Mark and Toby's lives who would take such a giant risk for them.

Other smaller screens directly in front of the operators were now showing various CCTV footage from areas near and around the prison where they had managed to track the three wanted men. The footage also showed the incompetence of the prison staff and first responders.

From the entrance to the room decked out in black and filled with men dressed in black came maybe the blackest of them all. Not only did he dress in black like all the others working for black ops, he had an extremely black heart and mind. There was nothing Dark Operative Terry Rickles wouldn't do for the win and nobody he wouldn't shoot in the back to get what he wanted, which was usually a promotion or more dirt to use against people.

"Quite the cock up," Terry said as he approached his underling, who was the same age as him. TFC said nothing, he knew how Rickles would play this and he knew that his place was firmly under the bus right now. "Do we know who did it?"

"No," The French Connection grunted.

One of the operators, who knew how to keep his job, had an ear open for everything the DO said and immediately put a close up of Paul's face onto one of the larger monitors on the wall for his superior to see.

"He doesn't look like much," Terry said, sounding almost offended that someone who wasn't built like the Terminator and armed to the teeth could have sprung the prisoners. "Skinny runt could certainly pass for one of your lot." Terry Rickles and The French Connection had served in several conflicts together at the same rank most of the time, although Terry had planned, plotted and fucked over enough people to rise to the top, while TFC had merely gotten on with the jobs given to him. TFC was a grafter, not a chaser, and Rickles knew that the man stood next to him didn't consider his current post to be true graft.

"I…" The French Connection paused to alter his direction and not attach the blame to himself "*we* can't be held responsible for this mess." He pointed at the toppled van, "Prison transport let this happen, it was out of our hands."

"That's where you're wrong," Terry turned his vulture-like head to look at the gruff operative. "They were your people being transported," he fought not to smirk yet. "You should have had men on the ground to ensure they arrived at the prison as intended." He shook his head while maintaining eye contact. "This is poor planning on your part." He turned back to look at the screens. "They should have still been in your hands, so to speak."

"Well, they'll be back in my hands soon enough," TFC said through teeth under so much pressure they could shatter at any moment. His eyes burned holes into the side of Rickles' head and his knuckles involuntarily clenched into rock-hard fists.

"So you have a lead?" Rickles asked condescendingly.

"Not yet," his eyes were about to pop out of their sockets.

"Well, what do you have?"

"They took off on foot," a low growl responded. "Clearly injured and unable to get very far," he said pointing a rigid finger at one of the monitors that showed the trio limping away from the scene of the crime.

"But you don't know where, do you?" The DO asked smugly. He already knew that the police had lost them almost immediately and that they hadn't been spotted on any other cameras since the initial escape. Either they knew the city well or they were very fortunate, probably both.

"They can't have got far—"

"They're gone," Rickles interjected before having to endure any bullshit oaths of capture within the hour or whenever. "Accept responsibility for your mistake and acknowledge that they're in the wind."

"You're not suggesting—"

"The department has wasted more than enough time and resources on these two pets of yours," Terry wanted no more back and forth on the issue and was only interested in assets that made them money, not cost them funding. The narcotics operations the department ran brought in big money and the two operatives his underling had been handling were good at selling vast quantities of their stolen drugs, but ever since the incident at the now infamous house they were liabilities and not earners. "Forget about them and move on."

"You can't be—"

"If they resurface you'll deal with them," he said as he stared coldly into TFC's hard eyes. "Otherwise, they're just a waste of department time and money." Rickles wasn't in charge because he had a habit of losing money for the military, it was because he ran a tight ship and acquired huge sums of wealth for them. "You have plenty more operatives to manage and duties that require your attention."

"I—"

"Move on!" the DO barked. "That's an order!"

Before TFC could say any more or punch him or worse, the DO turned 180-degrees before marching out of the Surveillance Room. The killer in a tobacco-tainted tie trembled with rage but managed to keep it in. He so badly wanted to kill Rickles, Mark, Toby and whoever the other junkie-looking cunt was, along with a whole host of prison staff and incompetent city police officers he could almost feel his blood burning the underside of his skin.

The operators all sat silently staring at the computer monitors and banks of screens. Save for the light emitted from the multiple video feeds, the room was in darkness. It still wasn't dark enough for TFC though, it wasn't black enough to hide his temper that was visible on the lines of his weathered face. He swore to himself that this wasn't over and that both Mark and Toby would pay dearly for this. He'd made them what they were – he'd taken them from petty street dealers to the big time and all under his protection. Now they were putting him in the position of weighing up whether he should assassinate Rickles or let him get away with thinking he could talk down to him the way he had.

Chapter 6 – Past

How It All Began

Seeing colours bounce and strobe while watching fellow students throw shapes on the dance floor was all perfectly fine and normal for any young Brit at the weekend. Seeing the colours meld together to then form new life forms that wave at you and pull strange faces was a whole other thing. Watching the other teenagers and young adults you attended university with mash together to create bizarre and sometimes grotesque-looking entities that flailed violently to the thumping sounds of bass and screeching treble was not normal.

Toby knew that his latest concoction had kicked in and was in the process of kicking his arse. The sweat poured from his body and created layer upon layer of thick, chemical-laced slime that dripped onto the tiled floor to form luminous puddles that twitched and rearranged into tiny shapes that were anthropomorphised before his eyes. At one point a miniature Lilo and Stitch rose from the lilac lake under Toby's table and then proceeded to hula dance together before exploding into rainbow icicles that momentarily pierced his flesh.

He blinked the pain and illusion away before wiping the sweat from his brow. He breathed deep and decided that a trip to the bathroom to splash cold water on his face would be a good idea. His shaky fingers reached out and supported his unsteady rise to his feet, but halfway to standing he freaked out at the sight of his grubby hand and questioned whose it was. The scream he emitted was unheard by anyone due to the loud music blasting all around him in the busy club, but a couple of the strangers he'd found himself sat with around the table saw him. Some nearby clubbers took a break from dancing and watched the stranger shiver upright and then wobble away, all the while making faces of an electroshock patient with no bit between their teeth.

The walk to the bathroom didn't get any better. Toby was bounced and shoved from dancer to post to table to disgruntled angry cunt who screamed and threatened him as he lurched onwards across the dancefloor towards his final destination. Fortunately for Toby he had been to the club numerous times and therefore the location of the bathroom was already known to him, so all he had to concentrate on was his footwork. His mind was filled with the simple command of 'put one foot in front of the other and keep your torso erect,' but these things didn't always occur at the same time. There were moments when he would regain focus and realise that he was simply standing. Nothing more, just standing with a perfectly straight posture at a random spot in the club. On he went.

Inside the toilets, Toby breathed a sigh of relief as soon as his hands rested on the edge of the basin. He knew he had made it to where he wanted to be and that in a moment cold water would be splashing his face and sobering him up, and then he screamed. The sight of his own reflection in the stained and streaked mirror was completely unexpected. For one, he thought he had momentarily stepped out of his physical form to then look at it from an ethereal plain, and second it looked like absolute dog shit that had been trampled by an overweight rugby team. After the screaming stopped he took deep breaths and reminded himself that the capsules he and Charlie had swallowed earlier in the evening were of a new breed of psychedelic that they had invented. He and Charles were always creating new chemical cocktails and using themselves as guinea pigs, nothing new there. What was different this time was his surroundings. Toby was not a sociable person, but Charles' girlfriend Michelle had insisted the pair accompany her and some friends for a night of drinking and dancing – neither of which Toby cared for. He was a man of science, or chemistry at least, not a typical student out for a good time on a Friday night. His 'good times' were either in a lab or in an empty room on his own while riding out the effects of what he'd cooked up in the lab.

More deep breathing was then followed by the necessary cold water on the face to try to snap him out of the grip of these weird new chemicals he'd ingested. He and Charles had been pushing their R&D further and harder than ever before until they had reached their current state of not really knowing what was truly in the pills and capsules they swallowed. He knew that if he went back through all of his notes he could list every single element of the make-up of what he was currently riding high on, but at that moment in time all he knew was that psilocybin, 2C-B, amphetamines and ergotamine had been prominent ingredients.

"These fucking pills ain't shit!" a loud and angry voice suddenly filled Toby's ears. The sound filled him with terror, not just because it was loud and angry, but also because this statement may well have been directed at him. Toby had sold a lot of students a lot of pills over the months and some of them were here in the club tonight.

"I stand by my work as a man of science damnit!" Toby blurted out at his own twisted reflection.

"They're the same as the last lot," another male voice said calmly.

"Then they're just as good," Toby responded with a waterfall of drool leaking from his mouth. He now realised he'd forgotten how to swallow.

"They're not the fucking same you dozy cunt!" a second angry voice barked.

"Nobody's getting buzzed from them," the first angry voice spoke again.

"Can't be my pills then," Toby said offended by the insinuation and confident he was right in his defence.

"People are just puking everywhere and fucking sweating a lot," the second angry voice spoke up.

"But no fucking come up!" angry voice one barked.

Toby could relate. He was sweating a lot too, and he also felt the need to hurl chunks into the bathroom sink and at everywhere else for that matter. Shit, maybe he and Charles had flogged some of the new gear to others during this trial period by mistake. Maybe he was strong enough to keep the barf at bay, but the average clubber would never be able to. Shit, no wonder these guys were angry. Toby then realised, before the fear could intensify, that he had absolutely no idea who the two angry voices were or who the third voice belonged to. Toby splashed more water on his face.

"What can I say boys?" the calm voice said suavely. "The youth of today, eh?" There was a slight chuckle.

The cold water helped Toby realise something very important; the voices weren't actually talking to him. In the mirror he could now focus on the background and saw that two giant bouncers kitted out in the usual black suit and white shirt were looming over another younger guy wearing stylish threads and a pair of gold Elvis Presley sunglasses.

"Are you winding me up?" one of the bouncers asked as he jabbed a finger into the younger man's chest.

"Is that supposed to be funny?" the second asked with a slight shove of the younger guy.

"Look boys, there's nothing we can do about it tonight," Mark said with a calm and reassuring tone and smile. "Tomorrow I'll go and see my guy—"

"Fuck tomorrow!" the first bouncer barked.

"Fuck your guy!" the second bouncer snarled.

"That ain't helping us get our fucking money tonight you cunt!" the first bouncer got right up into Mark's grill.

"Take it easy—"

He didn't have the chance to finish his sentence. Both bouncers grabbed him and proceeded to drag him out of the toilets with ease. They used his head as a battering ram to open the doors to both the bathroom exit and then the fire escape. Fortunately for Mark the club was on the ground floor so there were no stairs to be thrown down, just concrete to land face first on in the back lane behind the building.

"You know the fucking deal Mark," the first bouncer shouted. "You give us pills to flog and in return you get to punt powder and puff."

"We can—"

One of the second bouncer's big black toe-capped boots silenced Mark the moment it drove into his stomach.

"Now, as a favour to you we'll let you get off with a little warning and a tax tonight," bouncer one pointed down at Mark with a fat rigid finger.

"But tomorrow night you best have some proper fucking pills for us!" the wannabe football player shouted before practicing his punt a second time on Mark's gut. As he drew his foot back for a third strike a loud smash was heard behind them, drawing the bouncers' attention.

Toby crashed through the fire exit, arms spread wide in the hope of having something to use as support to keep him on his feet. He came to a halt and stared bug-eyed at the giant men in black. To Toby they looked like gargoyles come to life, all cracked stone and weathered surfaces.

"Party's back in there mate," the first bouncer said, again with his finger extended but now aimed at the building Toby had just staggered out of.

"I heard something about pills," Toby said, but when he did he couldn't control either the volume or speed of his voice, resulting in a strange modification of each syllable as if he was being listened to on an old cassette tape as it got chewed up by a shitty car stereo.

"Not tonight pal," the second bouncer shook his head in disbelief of the state that the new arrival was in. "Go back inside now, yeah?" He shooed him away with both hands like he was speaking to a small child.

"I know all about pills," Toby said with a twisted smile and two thumbs up. The bouncers closed their eyes and shook their heads. Surely it was in their power to eject idiots who tried to interact with them. Surely there was a line that, once crossed, meant the punter was too fucked up to stay and party. They'd been told by the management countless times that there was no such thing as 'too fucked to party.' As long as they were spending money and not hurting other people, punters could crack on.

"I fucking love pills," Toby smiled wider at Mark. "All pills," he blinked slowly, unsure if he was actually seeing Mark get to his feet or if it was just part of another illusion. "What you got?" he asked the floor. "What seems to be the problem with them?" His eyes trailed back up to Mark who was now stood directly behind and between the bouncers. "Talk to me boys." Toby stopped speaking at the sight of Mark smashing a fist into the side of the first bouncer's temple, instantly knocking him out. The second bouncer span around in shock, only to be met with the same fate.

Mark nodded confirmation to himself that both twats had been successfully dealt with as he looked down at their sleeping faces. Once satisfied they'd been taken care of he smiled at the stranger, who was clearly off his face, and stepped over them while removing the brass dusters from his knuckles.

"Cheers dude," Mark said with a charismatic smile. "Much appreciated."

"You're welcome," Toby smiled back. "What did I do?" He raised his eyebrows and tried to recall the last five minutes.

Mark chuckled before asking, "Did you say you're after pills?"

Toby   smiled   like   a   fat   kid   in   a   cake   shop.

The place was quiet and filled mostly with bar flies and the occasional student too fucked to get into any nightclubs. There was no music in there, just the low murmur of conversation in the background.

"These are fucking good pills you got dude," Toby stated with eyes like saucers. He was on another level now – no longer did his mind trip the light fantastic, he was alert and focused with a full body tingle. "What was the problem back at the club?" he asked before dislodging another few cocaine boulders from the back of his nasal passage and into his sticky throat by way of grotesque snorts.

"I punt the best pills myself," Mark explained, "but get cheaper ones to give to the doormen I bribe to let me sell at different venues." He smiled mischievously, "Turns out those pills were a bit *too* cheap."

"They could still be salvageable," Toby blurted. The idea of bad pills, or any other kind of bad drug, didn't sit well with him and he considered it his duty as a cook and chemist to ensure all narcotics were of the highest calibre before reaching the end user. "With the right bit of alchemical know-how." Toby cocked his head to say, *why not?* Anything was possible in his lab.

"And you know alchemy do you?" Mark raised his eyebrows dismissively.

"When it comes to chemicals," Toby swallowed some more bitter lumps, "especially drugs," his eyes watered a little, "nobody knows as much as me." He took a swig of his bottle. "Well, maybe Charles, but he specialises in downers more than anything else."

"Who's Charles?"

"My classmate, old friend and fellow dope fiend," Toby said proudly.

"You guys study chemistry together?"

"Yep. Both top of the class. First-class honours apiece. Brightest and best of the bunch."

"What's your name dude?" Mark said with a smile. He liked this guy. Sure, he was weird and smelled pretty rotten, but he liked him anyway.

"Toby."

"Toby, I'm Mark." A fist was extended to bump. "When can you look at these pills for me?" *Time for business*, he thought.

"Shit, right now dude," Toby said seriously.

Mark wasn't sure what Toby was thinking or how he intended on checking the pills, but he decided to trust the weirdo anyway. He retrieved the carrier bag, which was still filled about a quarter full, and passed it under the table to Toby. After retrieving one of the pills, Toby studied it above the table for a moment and then dabbed the tip of his tongue against it a few times.

"Shit," Toby said bluntly, "but not completely useless. I'll need to take them to the lab and add a little something-something, then they'll be sending the end user to outer-fucking-space!" He jumped up out of his chair and whistled through his teeth with his arms clamped to his sides as he did a space rocket impression.

Mark laughed at the madman before him, and then almost snorted his bourbon and coke back out through his nose when the rocket lost balance and fell back into his chair.

"You can tell that just from a single lick?" Mark asked, still not completely convinced by the chemist's boasts.

"Of course," Toby said as he adjusted himself in the seat, "I'm a genius."

"A genius?"

"Nobody knows drugs like I know drugs," Toby stated very seriously. "Nobody!" He pointed a finger in Mark's direction but not actually at him and frowned at the idea of such a thing.

Mark thought for a moment. Obviously Toby was fucked-up on gear – his bumbling back at the club with the bouncers had proven that – but now he seemed to be talking lucidly and with confidence. And not a coked-up confidence either, an actual genuine confidence that people had when their shit stank right. Mark leaned closer and raised his eyebrows, saying, "Prove it."

The cook returned the raised eyebrows and smiled.

Toby had cut himself a set of keys for each and every one of the laboratories on the campus almost as soon as he enrolled. He and Charles had clicked on day one and not long after they knew that private access to all the university had to offer must be obtained. They had each set about stealing keys from the cleaners, copying them and then leaving them laying around somewhere the cleaner would find. They figured that this way it simply looked like they had misplaced the keys rather than lost them or had them stolen, which would have forced the administration to change all the locks. Being spotted by security cameras wouldn't be an issue as long as nothing was damaged or destroyed. To the lazy security guards who might glance at a monitor displaying Toby or Charles entering the lab it would look like nothing more than a research technician using the facilities at a slightly odd hour – nothing to get up off your arse for.

As always, at this time of night there was no fear of discovery by anyone. It was late on a Friday, so all of the students, faculty and staff would be out getting pissed or already passed out due to the effects of alcohol. Toby, still feeling the consequences of both the alcohol and drugs he'd taken earlier, swayed on his feet while stood at the counter next to Mark, who sat and studied his new friend.

Toby worked by the light of a single naked bulb, insisting that switching on the room's main lights may attract attention from unwanted eyes. Mark didn't mind the clandestine nature of it all, but he did worry that the chemist would mess his alchemy up due to not being able to see what the fuck he was doing. Toby squinted through one eye at the label on another bottle, moving it closer and then further away and then back again in an attempt to read the tiny letters.

"Do you actually know what you're doing?" Mark had to ask. He'd been watching Toby fuck around with liquids, pills and Bunsen burners for almost an hour now and was yet to see anything that looked like real progress.

"Don't question my talent with narcotics dude," Toby said sternly, belching mid-sentence. "My ability to stand is somewhat questionable at the moment, but my knowledge is sound." And with that he staggered sideways and then back again, bumping into Mark to stop his trajectory. Once he felt balanced he took some litmus paper from a packet in a draw and rubbed it over one of Mark's pills. After inspecting the colour through squinting eyes he grabbed one of the glass bottles containing a clear liquid that he had prepared earlier and took a sniff. Toby's eyes bulged with the burning sensation from inhaling the contents and then he smiled at Mark. "Grab that container," he said nodding at a plastic bowl with a closed lid near to Mark.

Mark did as instructed in silence.

"Put the pills in," Toby slurred.

Mark emptied his bag of crap pills into the now open bowl before seeing it taken from him by Toby, who proceeded to pour some of the foul-smelling contents of the glass bottle over the small ecstasy tabs within.

"Mix," Toby instructed.

Mark swilled the bowl around, ensuring all of the pills got coated in the liquid that gave off harsh fumes making him hold the bowl at arm's length. Once all of the pills had been covered Toby motioned for Mark to put the bowl back down on the counter, "Now wait," the chemist said with a knowing nod.

"For how long?" Mark asked, as he looked around the lab for a clock. On the far wall he could just make out a circular clock bearing the time 01:20 in the am.

"Long enough to have a smoke," Toby answered.

"You blaze?"

"Do priests rape little boys?" Toby responded like it was the most natural thing in the world to say, which for Toby it was.

"What?"

"Roll this," Toby said with another belch as he handed Mark a small baggy of skunk from his pocket.

Mark opened the bag and took a giant inhale that almost knocked him off his perch. He considered himself to be a cannabis connoisseur, but he had never smelt gear that potent before.

"Fuck me!"

"I'm not gay," Toby cut Mark off before he could finish

speaking. He had just met Mark and couldn't be sure of his sexuality and felt that it was something that should be established early on so that there would be no misunderstandings later on down the line.

"What?" Mark had no idea why Toby had just brought sexuality into the conversation. He found it odd that he would suddenly throw it out there like that, and it suggested the guy had some insecurities in the matter, possibly his own leanings too. "I wasn't offering, I'm just saying," Mark held the baggy up "This gear is fucking stinky dude. It's—"

"Kryptonite."

"It's what?"

"Kryptonite," Toby explained. "I grow it. It's mine. Not even Charles can grow it," he said while doing a little jig and waving two middle fingers at an imaginary Charles.

"So, you grow your own bud and you make your own pills," Mark said as he started to roll a joint with the kryptonite. "I've never seen you flogging stuff around town though dude," Mark raised his eyebrows. "You just slinging to students on campus or what?"

"I don't sell, I smoke," Toby paused to think, "and snort and swallow."

"I thought you said you weren't pink," Mark said smiling slyly and looking over his sunglasses.

The pair chuckled.

"I just make drugs for me dude. And Charles. I'm not a dealer. Well, sometimes I am but in general I'm not. Not really. Just a friend of fiends who sometimes have an itch that can't be scratched elsewhere."

"You can manufacture in quantity though, yeah?" Mark's mind was already forming a business plan.

Toby nodded his confirmation.

"I'm always in the market for new supplies if you're interested," Mark said. As far as he was concerned, even if Toby couldn't salvage the pills, he had primo green and that could make money.

"How much you need?" Toby was immediately thinking that

this could be a good excuse for him to experiment even more than he already was with his chemical shenanigans. "And of what?" He loved to invent and improve upon narcotics, so having someone who could then sell them in quantity would mean that he would have regular feedback from the average user and not just two super-fiends like himself and Charles or the occasional student who was just grateful to be getting anything in the first place.

"As much as you can make of whatever you can make. There's a market for everything dude. I can sell snow to Eskimos."

"Really?" Toby was a little too wasted to appreciate that Mark was just exaggerating for the sales pitch. He stopped and wondered for a moment why Eskimos would want to purchase snow.

"Just look into my eyes," Mark said with an award-winning smile. Toby leant forwards and tried his damnedest to focus. When he did finally manage to see clearly he only saw his own reflection staring back at him from the black shades framed in gold.

"I can't see your eyes," Toby confessed.

"What can you see?"

Toby struggled harder with the task of looking forwards. He squinted and strained, focused and refocused between moments of blurred hazes until eventually he saw something. He dismissed it at first, figuring Mark was speaking metaphorically about his own reflection, but then he recalled something from pop culture and said out loud, "T-C-B."

"I always do," Mark said with a confidence and charm that even   Toby   was   not   impervious   to.

Mark had to respect how calm Toby was in the passenger seat. Sure, he may have been too high to truly comprehend what was going on around him or to truly appreciate the danger he was in, but still his lack of reacting like a little bitch went down well with the driver of the car travelling at close to triple digits through built-up urban areas. He rested one hand on the steering wheel while smoking a cigarette with the other, all the while chatting casually to his passenger.

Toby didn't really care. Sure, he knew they were going fast and that Mark should be gripping the wheel with both hands while focusing more on the road, but it was still much safer than if he was driving.

"Those pills were fantastic," Mark said nodding. There'd been some polite chit-chat once he'd picked Toby up from the campus, but now he needed to get down to business. Toby said nothing, he just nodded confirmation like it was obvious that the pills would be fantastic after he'd played with them in the lab a little. "And that fucking skunk..." Mark's words trailed off as he shook his head in disbelief. There were no words to describe how high the Kryptonite had got him. He was a seasoned smoker, but that shit had been fucking mental to say the least. Mental just didn't do it justice in Mark's opinion but he couldn't think of anything better.

"I know," Toby said with a cocky smile. Of all the narcotics he'd developed, Kryptonite was his favourite. That was his legacy and what he would be remembered for after he died.

"I have a plan," Mark stated. "We should partner up."

"I already told you I'm not gay," Toby said with a shake of the head.

"You cook it. I sell it," Mark said ignoring the homosexual jesting.

"Cook?"

"Cook, grow, manufacture, mix," Mark shrugged as he hurled the speeding car around slower traffic. "However you do it," – he didn't need to drive fast, he just did – "I can sell anything you can make that gets people off their faces." He looked at Toby and nodded solemnly to show how serious and honest he was being.

"And we can make a lot of money together," he looked back at the road and swerved to narrowly avoid other cars. "Easy."

"I'm no dealer dude," Toby almost spoke to himself when saying this. He'd sold a little here and there at the uni plenty of times, but deep down he knew he wasn't right for the task. "I'm just a chemistry student who likes to get high. Or low sometimes." Toby thought for a second, "Or both."

"I'm not asking you to deal," Mark already knew that that was his specialty and he could see Toby was lacking in particularly spectacular people skills. "I'll do the dealing. You just give me the shit to sell."

"But what shit do you want exactly? Kryptonite isn't for sale, that's my own personal strain."

"I don't think the rest of the smoking community is ready for that stuff dude," Mark shuddered at the thought of supplying some of the part-time tokers he dealt with trying to wrap their heads around that kind of a high. "It would make you a lot of cash though," he thought out loud. "There ain't nothing else as strong as that about."

"I don't have the space for bigger grow ops," Toby thought about the small space he had found in the attic of one of the older sections of the university. Apart from the size and the need for him to run cables into it for electricity, it was ideal. The building was located away from the rest of the campus and barely saw any people going in or out of it. The structure had been deemed unsound by the council, but the university board wanted to keep it for heritage reasons. Toby used it for illegal ventures. "I'm just about growing enough to meet my own needs," he said picturing the dozen or so giant plants he had currently in flower.

"I can get you grow space, that's not a problem." Mark said this like it was the easiest thing in the world to find places to grow weed, and for him it was. "But it's pills and powders I really want dude."

"No psychedelics?"

"I can flog that too, but pills and powders are what the masses are yearning for." Toby could almost see the pound signs in the driver's sunglasses. "Pills and powders are how we make the pounds and pence."

"What pills and powders do you want?"

"They don't need to be specific dude," Mark smiled at his new partner. He knew now that Toby was on board. "As long as they give the customer the desired effect, they'll sell." He decided to break it down simply for the chemist. "At the weekend people wanna go up. Start of the week they go down. Middle of the week it's a mixed bag. Some want more energy, some wanna forget it ain't the weekend yet, others wanna be happy—"

"I get the idea," Toby said nodding.

"So, can you supply and are you interested in getting paid?" Mark asked almost rhetorically at this point.

"Sure," Toby answered immediately. "I love drugs," he stated matter-of-factly. "I love making them almost as much as I love taking them."

Mark flicked the cigarette butt and then offered his hand to shake, "Partners?"

"Partners," Toby said shaking the driver's hand. They exchanged smiles before Toby continued, "Tell me about this grow space. How big is your pad?"

"My pad?" Mark asked surprised. "You can't grow at my place dude, the halls of residence are far too small and indiscreet for that."

"Halls of residence?" Toby was now very confused. "Wait, you're a student?!"

"Fuck yeah I'm a student," now Mark was confused. "What you think I was?"

"A drug dealer."

"I do that too."

"Which uni do you go to? What subject do you study?" Toby was blown away by this latest revelation. There was nothing student-like about Mark. He screamed cool, not intellectual. Money, not books. A whiff of debauchery, not academia.

"Economics and philosophy," Mark said casually. "Joint honours at Cardiff University."

"Huh," Toby said lost in his thoughts about how wrong he'd

been by Mark's outward appearance and self-sure attitude. Most of the students Toby met acted and looked like students. Of course there were confident students who had life experience, but Mark exuded this on a whole other level. "So dealing's just a side hustle for extra cash?"

"I'd say it's the other way around at this stage," Mark confessed. "Most of the lecturers don't even know who I am." He tried to remember the last time he'd actually attended a lecture or seminar, but couldn't recall with accuracy.

"Aren't you worried about getting kicked out?"

"Uni's a breeze dude," Mark almost laughed at the thought of worrying over something as trivial as exams. "And like I said the other night, I always take care of business."

"So how are you going to take care of grow spaces?"

"I got women all over town who would be more than happy to let us grow at their pads in exchange for some merch," Mark said it casually like he was talking about borrowing a cup of sugar.

"You've got women all over town? Who are you, Super Fly?" Toby wanted to tell himself that Mark was full of shit and just telling tall tales to impress him, but deep down he could feel it: Mark didn't try to impress anyone, he genuinely lived this life.

Mark smiled at his new partner while overtaking some slower moving cars on the busy high street, "You ever want a little strange I'll hook you up partner," he paused to wiggle his eyebrows and show more teeth behind the smile, "free of charge."

"You're a pimp too?!" Toby yelled.

"Not exactly," Mark laughed. "Women do like to make me happy though." His mind wandered to images of himself in long mink coats down to alligator shoes and hats with feathers protruding from the brim resting on his shaved head. He then realised he'd probably need to grow his hair to pull the look off properly.

"A pimp and a dealer! Who the fuck are you?" Toby yelled louder with a mixture of shock and excitement born from now being partnered with the man driving the car.

"Just another dude trying to get by," Mark said casually as he stepped on the gas and the car took off at even more dangerous speeds   through   the   urban   landscape.

As far as Mark was concerned, a beautiful woman was a beautiful woman regardless of age, race, size, shape or anything else. He had accumulated a lot of experience when it came to the subject of women, and not just beautiful women either.

This particular woman was twice his age but fucked with the energy and determination of a pro-athlete. She had thrown him on the bed and used him for hours, which he had loved every second of. He couldn't remember her name, every time she had told him he had been distracted by the size of her breasts. She had the figure of a porn star, and as far as Mark was concerned could have easily made a career as one and earned awards for it.

At the front door to her house he gave her one more deep kiss and squeeze of arse before leaving with a spring in his step. It had been a good night and an easy morning. Some women get clingy after good dick, but this one didn't. She hadn't so much as asked for his number; Mark even suspected she didn't remember his name either. That was a great night in Mark's opinion, two complete strangers using each other for sex and then parting ways with no fuss or drama. *Today was going to be a good day*, he told himself.

Memories of how he'd been ridden and slobbered over filled his mind's eye as he got in the car and stuck his key in the ignition, and then he saw it. In the back seat was the shape of someone or something that shouldn't have been there. Mark let go of the key protruding from the ignition and went for the door handle, but the sudden intrusion of a gun muzzle in his peripheral stopped him cold. Mark had no experience with firearms but it was clear even to him that it was the barrel of a pistol that now filled his eyesight to the side and blocked out whoever was sitting in the back seat and threatening to shoot him in the face.

"Don't move," a deep and gruff voice commanded. He spoke with authority and confidence. The tone of the voice made it very clear that any refusal to comply with orders would meet with a swift and lead-infused death right there in the driver's seat. As Mark sat frozen in place with one hand on the door and the other on the steering wheel he picked up on the stink of cigarettes and alcohol. Someone smoking at this time of the day was nothing to worry about, but whisky-tinged breath at this hour in the morning was something to be aware of and take into account when speaking or making decisions. Only fiends and alcoholics drink whisky for breakfast. "We need to talk, Mark Anthony King." The use of his full name immediately made Mark rethink the natural assumption that it was a rival drug dealer or disgruntled customer sat in the back of his car. When you deal drugs there's always a good chance you're going to step on someone's toes or not satisfy an overly greedy bouncer, but those kinds of people seldom break into your car with a pistol and then address you by your full name. "I would apologise for the dramatics, but they are necessary." There was only one more semi-feasible option left in Mark's mind.

"I swear I didn't know she was married," he said unconvincingly.

"Of course you did," said the stranger. "I'm sure that even helped you get off." The voice didn't so much contain anger, rather judgement.

"If you're going to punish someone for this, surely it should be—"

"I'm not the slag's husband."

Mark thought for a moment. A rival dealer would have already shot him or at the very least threatened to shoot him by now. The guy said he wasn't married to Mark's late night encounter, so what else was there?

"Brother?" he asked confused *"Father?"* Mark asked hesitantly, slightly concerned at how old he would have to be if he was the father of the cougar he'd fucked the night before.

"I'm here with a proposition for you," the man in the back said. "Don't adjust the mirrors. We'll talk as you drive."

"Drive where?"

"Doesn't matter," the man said as he took the gun out of Mark's eyeline.

Mark slowly turned and faced front before starting the car. He glanced around at the car's mirrors and saw that they had all been angled so that he couldn't see into the back seat. He decided not to wait for further prompting or instructions and pulled out into the road and began what he knew may well be his last drive.

"I've been watching you for a while," the voice explained.

"Hey man, if this is some homosexual thing then just shoot me now because I don't play like that." It was at this point Mark thought of another alternative to who the mystery passenger may be. He suddenly realised that this could be some gay stalker who'd had his eye on him for some time and had finally given up on waiting and decided to just take Mark by gunpoint. He'd had female stalkers in the past, so why not a homicidal homosexual?

"This is about your other two favourite things in life," said the stranger. This confused Mark even more as it implied one of his favourite things was cock, and not his own either. "Money and drugs," the mystery man stated coldly.

"You have my full attention," Mark said jauntily. Until now he had been half in the conversation and half in his thoughts of who could be in the back, but now the magic words had been spoken and Mark wanted to listen to every syllable.

"You recently started a partnership with a chemistry student," the words from the stranger sent a jolt down Mark's spine. "One Toby Jones," the new words sent new shivers to the point of almost causing Mark to shit in his tapered jeans. The man had been watching Mark for some time and knew a lot more than he should have from just casual observation. This was something different. "This has the potential to be a lucrative partnership with a little guidance and help."

"So you supply?" Mark asked cautiously. His initial deduction had been partially correct – the guy wasn't a rival but he was in the game.

"Yes."

"Supply what exactly?" Mark felt like he was talking to himself and had to question his sanity and whether or not he'd taken too much of something the night before and was now tripping hard balls. It was surreal, driving around aimlessly having a conversation with someone you couldn't see and didn't know, yet they seemed to know a whole hell of a lot about him.

"I will supply you with any and every illegal narcotic available on the streets," the voice said in a matter of fact tone.

"How? Are you a cook?"

"Not even close," the man sounded like he had been insulted by this but was trying to disguise his contempt. "All you need to know is that I can get my hands on whatever you can sell and I can get as much of it as you want."

"I think I'll need to know a bit more than that," Mark said with raised eyebrows. This smelled like a set up. He was now starting to get a waft of swine from the back of his ride. The gun had fooled him at first. The whole clandestine nature of the conversation had worked well for a while, but now he felt that twinge in his gut that told him authorities were somehow involved.

"Mark, listen to me and listen well. I am offering to make you an extremely wealthy man. I am offering to supply you and your partner with enough narcotics to flood the streets for years to come." The voice sounded almost angry that they were making this proposal, like the man was being forced into having this conversation with Mark. "In exchange for this, you will give me half of the money you bring in."

"Half?!" Mark yelled. He would have turned to see if the stranger was smiling or laughing behind his back, but he had to drive and not get shot.

"Yes, Mark: half."

"But we'll be taking all the risk and—"

"I can help with that too," the man said it like the authorities were absolutely nothing to be concerned about.

"How?"

"Let me be clear with you. If you agree to this arrangement, there will be many questions you have that I won't give you answers to. This will very much be a need-to-know deal and only I will determine what you need to know. Am I clear so far?"

Mark nodded his head 'yes' in confirmation of understanding all that the stranger had just told him and inside he knew that this was going to be big. Earlier thoughts of rival dealers, cheated husbands or undercover police vanished. Mark was well educated in the ways of drug dealing and drug trafficking. He had studied his peers and predecessors. He had heard all about

'Freeway' Ricky Ross and the Nicaraguan Contras cocaine trafficking. Now, here he was: just a lowly street dealer in South-fucking-Wales who had just made a government connection for major supplies of drugs. You could practically hear the fanfare in his head like when you hit the jackpot on a fruit machine.

"Once a month you and your partner will meet me to resupply and update me on anything that I need to know. Still clear?"

"Crystal." *Ching-ching-ching-ching-ching.*

"So long as you sell only from the house that we agree on, there will be no need to fear the police turning up," again the man spoke like the law was nothing to be concerned about. This made Mark sure that whoever the stranger was, he was above the police and had some serious clout.

"Who the fuck are you man?"

"All you need to know is that working for me will make you very rich and that there will be no problems from the police," there was a slight pause and the faint sound of a sigh. "As long as you do nothing stupid."

"You expect me to just believe some complete fucking stranger who appears in the back of my car and—"

The sound of the hammer being pulled back to ready the pistol now at Mark's right temple silenced him quickly.

"I have one yes or no question for you Mark Anthony King," again there was a pause before the stranger asked, "Are we in business?"

Mark could tell from not only the bizarre situation he found himself in, but also the tone of voice and way that the man in the back of his car spoke that if he said no, it would be the last thing he ever heard. His death would be loud, quick and painless, but it would be final. Thoughts of all this being some set-up or elaborate hoax by Toby raced through his mind, but there was also that unrelenting feeling nagging at him and insisting that the person in the back of the car sounded serious. They didn't sound like a bullshitter or the kind of person who fucked around for the fun of it. Mark decided that this was no shit: all of it must be for real.

"Yes," he replied coolly.

The pistol was decocked and moved away from the side of the young driver's head.

"Wise decision," the man said before tossing a bulging Manila envelope onto the passenger seat.

"In there are all the documents and IDs you and Toby require. There are bank accounts, drivers' licenses and other paperwork you'll need to start renting a house. Make sure it's out of the town centre, somewhere residential, something plain and regular. Once you and your partner have found somewhere you're happy with contact me and I'll check it. If it meets with my approval you will proceed with the rental, but only after I give you the all clear. Do you understand?"

"Yeah, I hear you."

"Good," the voice sounded like the stranger was fed up with speaking to him. "Now pull over."

Mark did as instructed. He glanced around and saw that they were on a quiet residential street on the outskirts of town. He hadn't really been paying attention to his surroundings as he drove as the sound of winning slot machines in his head was very distracting.

"Put the mirrors back in position," instructed the stranger.

As soon as the wing mirrors and rear view mirror were back where they should be, Mark saw the owner of the surly voice. A middle-aged white guy in a black suit and tie. *Jesus-fucking-Christ*, Mark thought to himself, *this fucking guy even dresses like a shady spook*. The dealer then mulled over the idea that if the guy had let himself be seen in the first place this could have gone far smoother as he looked like a G-man doing dodgy shit.

"Along with the IDs and paperwork you'll find a mobile phone with my number already stored in it. Just speed dial one, it's the only number saved. Keep it that way. That phone is just for contacting me," his cold grey eyes almost pierced the rear-view mirror he stared so hard at the driver, "...and I mean nobody else." The man continued to stare at Mark, almost threatening to kill him using just his eyes. "When I get out of the car you'll wait here for five minutes before leaving. Don't try to follow me. Let Toby know that you have a new supplier and that the two of you will be moving in together."

"What if he doesn't go for it?" Mark asked without really thinking. "We haven't exactly known each other for very long."

"You're the salesman," the voice said almost mockingly. "Sell him on it."

This labelling of Mark as the salesman made him feel even more uneasy and caused the sounds of winning jackpots to cease. It sounded almost like a direct quote from a conversation he had had with Toby. It sounded like the stranger had Mark bugged in some way or another.

The stranger opened the door closest to the pavement and started to slide out of the stationary car.

"Call me when you find a house," were the man's parting words, and with that the door was closed and Mark was alone.

The driver then noticed how tightly he gripped the steering wheel. He realised how he was almost not breathing at all. He saw how well he handled a gun in his face. He reconfirmed with himself that today was indeed a good day.

"How long before you're up and running?" asked the man in black.

Mark looked at Toby for an answer. He had done most of the legwork getting them the place, but Toby would be the one manufacturing and growing so he had had the final say on the property and would determine when they would be open for business.

The house had turned out to be a semi-detached in a middle-class neighbourhood mostly full of pensioners. The type of place where you never saw children or litter on the streets. Many of the front gardens around the close were covered in pristine green nature but there were no pedestrians to be seen. Mark had concerns about this, but their new supplier had insisted that this type of location was better than somewhere in the heart of the city. After all he'd heard from the sullen character so far, Mark had to guess that having them set up shop out here would make it easier for surveillance of some kind. He tried to tell himself that this would mean him and Toby doing a lot of acting and pretending to be professional drug dealers, but really he knew that he and his partner were fiends right down to their very cores and it wouldn't be long before this house was a place of madness and mayhem fuelled by any and every narcotic known to man, and then some new ones the chemist would concoct for them too.

"It'll be a few months," Toby answered their supplier. "Setting up the grow room won't take long, but plants need time to—"

"You can start sooner," the older man cut Toby off like he was beneath him in rank. "I'll supply you with everything you need." The man stared icy cold at Toby, a stare that the chemist was all too familiar with. He always seemed to bring out the worst – and most violent – in people. "Anything you make later down the road is extra profit for the two of you," he grimaced at the pair of them as he said this. "You sell what I give you now though and you don't miss the monthly payment." He leaned forwards, "Ever!"

"Now let me tell you something, mister whatever-the-fuck-your-name-is, I don't take orders from no cun—"

The sight of the semi-automatic pistol with a silencer already attached to the barrel made Toby stop talking. When the stranger chambered a round and then pointed it in the chemist's direction he wished he didn't breath so loudly or indeed even exist so loudly. He feared that the very vibrations of his existence would be enough to warrant a wet work-style execution right here in the unfurnished living room of their new home and business.

"Make no mistake about it boys, you work for me now. I supply, you sell. You don't fuck up, I don't kill you." He pointed the pistol back and forth between the pair. "Simple," he stated coldly.

"Anything I put my name to better be of the finest fucking quality!" The words came from Toby but he didn't know why, and he found it hard to conceive of why on Earth he would dare to mouth off to the guy with an ice cold stare and what appeared to be a fully loaded and perfectly working pistol in his hand. "I don't make shit and we don't sell shit!" Again, more words that Toby had trouble recognising as his own.

Mark almost took a full step away from his new partner in order to avoid any of his blood splattering him when the grumpy cunt holding the gun used it on him. The only thing that stopped him was the fear of the movement being interpreted as hostility and the gun then being used on him.

"The quality is of no concern to me, just the money you make from selling it. If you need to improve the product that's on you. I'll supply you with whatever I have."

"So you're not making it." Mark made the stranger aware that he had shown some of his hand.

"This is one of them need-to-kno—"

"He's a fucking tax man!" Toby didn't hold back from yelling what he thought the stranger's hand was. "That's why he—"

"That does make sense," Mark agreed and suddenly realised just how fucking high he and Toby must be. The fact that they were now openly speaking their thoughts out loud meant that the shit they'd swallowed earlier was well and truly working. "But how does he know our full names?" Mark asked himself more than Toby.

"Dude, that ain't too difficult if you're willing to do some digging," Toby started speaking like it was just him and Mark in the room and as if the armed stranger didn't exist.

"That shit's risky man," Mark said with a rub of his shaved head. "If we're flogging other dealers' gear it could come back on us."

"It won't."

"Who the fuck are you man?" Toby couldn't take it anymore – he needed to know and so challenged the man. His mind dropped in and out of reality, but every time it hit the real world that question was there waiting for him with a loaded gun in its hand.

"*Need to know.*"

"I NEED to know!"

"I got it!" Mark exclaimed, causing the other two occupants of the room to stop and stare. "You're with the fucking government." He'd been thinking this since that first encounter in the back of his car, but the drugs in his system were what prompted him to say it out loud.

"No fucking way!" Toby yelled back at Mark.

"Think about all the documents and shit dude."

"I should have thought about that sooner – you're fucking right man," Toby nodded and smiled, happy that they had figured the mystery out. "He's a G-dude, a fucking government stooge."

"I'm not government," the stranger said. He was fed up and needed this encounter to end soon before he terminated both of the young men.

"You're something like that," Mark said confidently, "I know it."

"You're some kind of sneaky fucking thieving cunt and—" Again Toby was silenced by the pistol being aimed at his face.

"So help me God, I'll end this fucking business enterprise right here and now if you don't shut up!"

There was near silence in the room, save for the faint sounds of the stranger's teeth grinding and his finger tensing on the trigger. In Toby's head there was anything but silence. His mind was filled with a terrified scream at the sight of a gun pointing at him. After a few moments the screaming stopped due to the pistol being put back in the man's black coat.

"Get things ready for business ASAP," the stranger walked out of the room and shouted back over his shoulder, "I'll call you to collect your first pick-up in a week," before shutting the front door behind him.

There was more silence as both Mark and Toby contemplated the situation they found themselves in. Mark had decided 'fuck it, take a chance' and either make a boatload of cash or deal with whatever comes his way. What else was he going to do? Live a normal life? *Fuck that!*

Toby wasn't so sure. For the chemistry student there were many benefits of course, but he wasn't really one for shady business dealings and clandestine operations with unknown sources, he was just a drug enthusiast; no more, no less.

"I don't know about this shit man," Toby confessed. "What the fuck are we getting into?"

"We're taking care of business dude," Mark smiled coolly before strolling casually out of the room.

"I *really* don't know about this man," Toby started to shake his head and flail his hands. "That guy gives me the creeps. You see how quick he was to threaten to shoot me? He'd kill us in an instant. No hesitation. No regrets." Toby waited a moment for a response but got none. "And what the hell do we know about him? He knows fucking everything about us! He's just some mystery man in a suit with drugs, *which we haven't even seen yet,*" Toby paused again, but this time to recall something. "He's like that fucking movie dude, The French Connection." Again, Toby paused for a response. "Mark?" Silence. "Mark?" Only silence.

Mark was almost in awe of what he now stood and stared at. It could have just been the Kryptonite that he was blazing, but he was fairly confident that it was in fact the insane construction before him that had him staring in silence like he was some critic at an art gallery, taking in every minutiae and not really understanding most of it. Toby had been working in front of him for hours now, adding more pieces of glassware and adjusting different parts, linking various items and all the while taking hits on the joints that Mark kept rolling one after another. The spliffs had made it difficult for Mark to do much more than stand, roll, smoke and stare. He had considered getting a chair to sit on, but the thought of that kind of manual labour really didn't appeal to him at the moment. The Krypt really was kicking his arse, and he loved it.

Toby retrieved the last item of Pyrex and rested it gently onto a metal frame that held it above a Bunsen burner before stepping back, nodding an approving smile and retrieving the burning biff from his single audience member.

"What the fuck is all this dude?" Mark finally managed to ask.

"Trust me," Toby said between puffs, "I know we blew a lot of cash on this set-up, but the pills and powder will be top notch." Toby began waving his hands and pointing at random parts of the giant apparatus he had built over almost half of one side of the kitchen. The tubes, cylinders, containers, bowls and pipes of multiple sizes and shapes made mostly of glass and Pyrex ran everywhere and made Mark think about Jackson Pollock's art, but without the colour added to it yet. "Plus, when it comes to the quality of whatever crap TFC supplies this will help us get it up to healthy standards."

"Healthy?"

"I only take top-quality drugs dude," Toby spoke with an air of sophistication as if he was some wealthy dignitary with a pinkie held aloft and not the dope fiend dressed in faded joggers full of blim burns that he actually was. "I will only sell top-quality drugs too."

"I got no problem with that. So you're gonna grow weed in the attic and make pills and powder here in the kitchen, yeah?"

"Yep," Toby answered with a huge grin. The grow room he'd set up in the attic was the kind of thing he'd been dreaming of for years, only a little smaller.

"What pills are you going to make?"

"Charlie and I developed our own. We got narcs that can send the end user in any direction they want to go. We can just tell them they're X and Xanies, whatever, but the truth is they're all originals. We'll give our customers the effect they want, but only with the shit I make."

"And the man's shit?" Mark asked, slightly concerned that his partner was forgetting this crucial element of their set-up.

"I'll test it and then decide. Obviously, real cocaine and heroin can't be made by these fair hands, but alternatives can."

"You got no problem flogging H?"

"None," Toby replied immediately. "You?"

"No," Mark said after a few seconds contemplation. "Fuck it, whatever the people want, right?"

"For me, drugs are drugs dude," Toby said nonchalantly. "I'll make acid and other psychedelics, but again we can test and then sell whatever TFC gives us."

"You're really stuck on this French Connection name," Mark said with a grin.

"I can't just call him 'psycho cunt,' can I? Especially not within earshot."

The two stared in silence at the transparent spaghetti masterpiece before them. It twisted and turned in every direction, all ready to create chemical compounds of craziness for the insatiable masses.

"Life's about to get strange," Mark said with a smile.

"Take these, they'll help," Toby responded while fishing out some pills from his pocket and dropping two into Mark's open palm.

Mark swallowed the tabs before asking, "What were they?"

"Ups," Toby answered and then swallowed two himself. "I think."

Chapter 7 – Present

How It Ends

Luckily for Mark the road signs were in English, so following them to Antwerp was easy enough. The latest one informed him that they were less than 100 miles away from their destination. He cruised at a regular speed and felt no urges to put his foot down and drive in his usual lunatic style. Maybe it was the lack of a plan or the lack of a desire to visit Belgium, but whatever the cause he was in no rush to reach the city he knew next to nothing about.

At his side Toby kept himself occupied by wearing all of the jewellery he'd stolen and then adjusting them and rearranging them to create ever more pointless patterns on his body with the accessories. Mark looked over at him and wondered if he knew he was covered in women's jewellery or if it was all the same to Toby, just bits of metal and rock that he couldn't care less about.

Toby saw Mark looking at him and then looked down at himself. He had now managed to squeeze every last stolen piece onto his body somewhere and looked ridiculous.

"You ever think that maybe we fucked up?" Toby asked while still looking down at his glittering arms and chest.

"Fucked up what? The heist?"

"Life," Toby said, more contemplative than depressed.

"How can you fuck life up dude? There's no set rules or agenda," his voice went up a few octaves. "No guidelines to follow, no guaranteed marker of success."

"We're driving a stolen car to Antwerp to flog stolen jewels."

"And?" Mark was truly shocked that Toby could feel this way.

"We went to university dude. You don't think that maybe we should be doing more with our lives?"

"More?!"

"Charlie was working for one of the biggest pharmaceutical companies in the world—"

"Until you killed him," Mark interrupted him, completely uninterested in where his partner was about to take this train of thought.

"Until I—" Toby snapped his head violently to the side in shock to look at his friend. "What the fuck do you mean, 'until I killed him'?!"

"You don't remember?"

"Charles was one of my best and oldest friends you cunt! I'd never—"

"Stick a needle in his chest loaded with adrenaline?" Mark again interrupted.

Toby thought back to that most morbid and fucked up of days that changed his life forever. "That was an accident!" he screamed.

"Look dude," Mark stopped fucking with his friend. "There is no set way to live life. You make of it what you will."

"I sometimes think we're making a mess of it," Toby said glumly.

"Really?" Mark still couldn't believe what he was hearing.

"I did time behind bars. I'm on the run. I've got bikers trying to kill me. I'm hiding from the British government, police, military and black operatives or whatever the hell TFC is," he shook his head. "Surely this ain't the right way to be living dude."

"Would you rather be working in an office five days a week on minimum wage for a boss you hate in a company that couldn't give a fuck about you?" Mark asked with a single raised eyebrow at Toby, who sat and silently pondered what he'd just heard. Toby knew the answer, but now it felt like a two-wrongs-making-a-right argument. "You're sitting in a stolen car, looking like a rap superstar covered in stolen jewels, on your way to fucking Antwerp to make a boat-load of cash. How many people have adventures like that in their mundane lives?"

"I'm not sure many people would want to…"

"We're outlaws, not office workers. Don't forget that my man."

"I think there may be a fine line between outlaw and fuck up dude," Toby said as he began to remove the jewellery slowly and unenthusiastically.

"What's really going on here? This ain't like you," Mark suspected he already knew the answer.

"I'm just—"

"Out of fucking gear! That's why you're being so fucking glum and melancholy with the dumb questions and statements."

"I'm—"

"One good spliff in you and then you'll be back to normal. Back to trash talking people who are slaves to the grind. Back to loving the outlaw life!"

Toby thought for a moment. He contemplated how maybe he was right and Mark was wrong, but then he imagined working in an office and the idea sent shivers through his rectum.

"You're right," Toby said with enthusiastic nodding. "I need drugs!"

Toby's face was scrunched up and his eyes were closed, his lips drawn back across his face and sloping down slightly. The drug abuser had never been a stunner and now in this grainy freeze frame of him, taken from the security camera outside the jewellers, he looked even weirder. Of course, the stupid jib he was pulling didn't help, but then the average swinging dick seldom does look cool, or even normal, when there's gunfire in close proximity to them and they are hiding in the getaway car.

The French Connection sat and stared at the face of his former worker, a person whom he had never liked or even respected. In his opinion, Toby was scum. A drug-making, drug-selling, drug-taking stain on society. Sure, he'd needed to use people like Toby in order to achieve the results that he had been ordered to get, but right down to his bones he had always hated the hippie and everyone like him. He had hated the task he'd been set of recruiting street dealers in order to supply them with narcotics to gather funding for covert missions. Once he had been the one being sent to carry out these unsanctioned assignments, but then he got older and proved his mental faculties were as sharply edged as his physical abilities so they gave him a desk and a computer. After decades of running and gunning through war-torn countries, slipping and sliding through shadows to assassinate in secret, dropping into danger zones undetected in order to kill and capture, they rewarded him with an office job. The cunts.

He blew another puff of smoke at the screen on his desk filled with Toby's face and then asked the analyst stood on the other side of the room, "Where?"

"Holland sir," the analyst answered with perfect posture and chin held up, "Amsterdam."

"Amster... I should have bloody known," The French Connection growled the words, wanting to scream, shout, swear and smash the monitor in front of him. *How could I have been so stupid?* he screamed internally. Of course the two biggest drug abusers the UK has ever known would go and hide in Amsterdam, the pot-head capital of Europe if not the world. "How old is this footage?"

"Two days sir," the analyst answered promptly. He knew that the senior officer in the room was not to be kept waiting or given a response that was unsure. He had a well-earned reputation as a miserable cunt who often physically attacked peers and underlings in the building.

"Do you have anything else?"

"The driver managed to lose the police before fleeing the city for an as yet unknown destination."

"Mark," he growled through his tense jaw.

"Sorry sir?" The analyst wasn't sure he'd heard correctly.

"That's both of the bastards! And in fucking Amsterdam of all places! Little shits probably thought it was funny, like hiding right under my goddamn fucking nose!" he yelled at the monitor and stood, barely stopping himself from putting his fist through the screen.

"I don't follow sir," the analyst took a shuffling step backwards.

"Shut up!" yelled the angry officer. "I need to go to Amsterdam immediately."

"But sir, they're no longer in Amsterdam..."

"What?" The French Connection looked at the younger man like he had just threatened to rape his daughter.

"We haven't finished retrieving all of the necessary footage yet, but early indicators show them headed for Belgium," the analyst squeaked.

The ex-soldier sat and thought for a moment.

"Of course," he said after deliberation. "They have diamonds to sell. They're heading for Antwerp." He knew that Mark and Toby weren't master criminals or heist men, but he figured at least one of them, probably Mark, would know that Antwerp is the diamond capital of the world. "Once you have an exact location for them in Antwerp let me know."

"Sir, we've already wasted more time on this than we should," the younger man said uneasily. "Rickles told you—"

"FUCK RICKLES!" The French Connection bellowed at the top of his lungs as he sprang back up onto his feet and almost over his desk, causing the young man to close his eyes and pray he wasn't about to have the shit kicked out of him or worse. "These two belong to me! Track them and report to me immediately!"

"Ye—"

"Get out! Get to fucking work! NOW!"

The analyst quickly left the room and was grateful he could do it conscious and in one piece.

The French Connection lit another cigarette and then sat and calmed himself before beginning to make the necessary arrangements for everything he would need in Antwerp, be it manpower, drones, satellite access or even a simple pair of binoculars. If he moved quick enough he could be across the water and away from Rickles before he ever knew a thing. Mark and Toby needed to be terminated, and that was that.

The streets and architecture reminded them of Amsterdam and Holland in general. Many of the pavements and roads had a flat cobblestone and brick look, but all grey and with patches of regular concrete. There were regular tram lines everywhere and the shops were mostly three storeys and either white or some shade of pastel.

Mark pulled the stolen car over to the side of a quiet street near some shops, the signs for which neither he or Toby could read. They lowered the windows and took in the afternoon air and ambience of their surroundings. Neither were impressed. To them it just looked like Holland except without the drugs and whores; a boring and lesser country for it.

"How you wanna do this dude?" Mark asked Toby.

"It can't be that hard," Toby shrugged. "We just go to a few different places, get some offers and then choose the highest one." He turned to Mark, "Simple, right?"

"We're punting stolen shit dude, it ain't gonna be as easy as that."

"I'm sure most of these fuckers are crooked," Toby said dismissively.

"I fucking guarantee you that they are, but that won't make it any easier for us." Mark shook his head, already feeling the tension from the task that needed to be done. "They'll make us grab our ankles every step of the way."

"Do you have any idea whatsoever what this shit is actually worth?" Toby pointed at the bag of stolen jewellery now resting on the back seat.

"Not a clue," Mark said with a shake of the head. "Don't even know what kind of rocks most of them are."

"They won't so much as spit before fucking us over," Toby said as he noticed a middle aged and slightly overweight woman walking by the car. He held his hand out of the window to get her attention. "Excuse me, do you speak English?"

"A little," the woman said as she stopped and eyed Toby suspiciously. He looked and, even from outside of the car, smelled like he hadn't washed in weeks, which was quite accurate.

"Where can I sell rings and shit?" he asked abruptly with no smile or charm. He could have asked her in French or Dutch if needed, but he decided to communicate in English.

"You want to sell shit?!" the woman screamed back at him with a look of disgust before spitting in his face and running away while muttering in Dutch.

Toby wiped the saliva from his cheek and pondered the idea that maybe he should have spoken in Dutch or French. Mark shook his head in disgust at the lack of effort made by his partner. Sure, they were both tired and hungry from the sudden and unexpected road trip but he knew that when dealing with ordinary members of the public appearances had to be maintained. Some sort of standard civility needed to be attempted.

"Still got it with the ladies I see," Mark smirked.

Toby slid down in the seat and wished he had some gear to smoke.

"Sorry to bother you," Mark suddenly yelled to another pedestrian on the other side of the street as he waved a hand. "Where's the jewellers around here?" he asked as a man in his 50s approached looking a little confused.

"*Jewellers*?" The man struggled to say the word.

"Yeah, to sell diamonds and... well, jewels." Mark smiled and considered momentarily retrieving a necklace or something from the bag in the back to show him.

"Yah," after a few moments of thinking the man smiled and nodded. "Yah, juweliers, yah, Diamantkwartier, yah?"

"Yeah, diamonds dude," Mark smiled and nodded back.

"Yah, Diamond Quarter," the man smiled even more proudly and triumphantly at his English skills. He then took out his smartphone and brought up a map. He proceeded to show Mark where their current location was and where the diamond quarter was situated.

"Sweet," Mark said with a smile, nod and thumbs up to the helpful native. "Cheers dude." He then started the car and waved back at the man who raised a hand and walked away. "Easy," Mark smiled at Toby as he headed off in the direction of the world's   most   famous   diamond   district.

Mark and Toby had chosen the place completely randomly. As far as they were concerned one jewellers was as good as another because they had no clue about what they were doing or who they were dealing with.

After entering one of the shops and telling the woman behind the counter that they were there to sell stones, they were directed to a man in a suit who was informed of their intentions. Without saying a word to the unwashed and ragged foreigners he led them through a door, metal detectors and security guards who patted them down, and then they were taken up a steep flight of steps to the first floor where they arrived in a huge open-plan office. The place had multiple tables and chairs, most of which were occupied by Jewish merchants. They all wore the traditional kippah on their heads and had long side-locks that framed their faces.

Mark and Toby were taken to one of the men sat at a table and then left to figure things out for themselves. The man reminded the outlaws of Danny DeVito, only with long hair and a beard. The jeweller smiled and waited to hear what the younger men had to say. He half-expected them to be thieves about to pull one of the world's worst armed robberies.

"Have a butcher's dude," Toby said with a smile as he gave up on waiting for any formalities and simply dumped the bag of stolen jewels on the desk before the seated man. "Best stones in town," Toby said before winking at Mark who stood next to him observing the fat man.

"Did you steal these?" the jeweller asked with raised eyebrows and a smirk.

"What?!" Toby yelped.

"No," Mark said with a look of concern, like he may actually be offended by the accusation.

"Come on," Toby did an obviously fake smile and laugh, "are you serious?" He nudged Mark with his elbow.

"Who keep jewels like this?" the jeweller prodded the bag with a pencil he took from behind his ear.

"It's less conspicuous," Toby chuckled.

"Think about it," Mark smiled suavely. "Fine suit and a bullet proof briefcase cuffed to your wrist is just begging for trouble."

"Yeah, ladies handbag, jeans and a pair of crap sunglasses, who'd know?"

"Is this a joke? Did Haekel put you up to this? That old dog..." the jeweller began to laugh out loud and slap the table.

"This ain't no joke dude," Toby waved his hands to indicate that the man should stop laughing and thinking like he was. "We're selling this shit. If not to you, then some other Yi—"

"We're legit," Mark stepped forwards and spoke over his soon-to-be-saying-some-racist-shit partner. "The stuff's legit," he gave his best innocent face. "Just give us a legit price."

The jeweller sat back in his leather chair and studied the two obviously out of place sellers. After a few moments he indicated to the chairs in front of his desk for Mark and Toby to sit in, which they did happily. He then retrieved an optical loupe and electronic weighing scale along with some gloves. He proceeded to look through the bag of stolen jewels.

"Boys, boys, boys," he said after less than a minute of rummaging. "Most of these aren't even diamonds."

"So?" Toby asked confused.

"This is the Diamond Quarter of Antwerp, not a pawn shop in Harlem."

"Come on, man," Mark said unimpressed with the fat man's tactics. "You don't just deal in diamonds."

"No?" the man asked sarcastically. "Then why call it the Diamond Quarter?"

Mark and Toby sat back and started to think that they had wasted their time and a new plan would be needed.

Happy that he had outfoxed the pair of idiots, the jeweller began taking items out of the bag and inspecting them more thoroughly.

"All right," the fat man said sighing, "let's see what we can see." He inspected each item through the loupe with carefully placed gloved hands. "You see boys," he spoke softly as he worked, "I've been here in the Diamond Quarter for a very long time. Not since the beginning of course, no. Diamantkwartier is the oldest diamond district in the world despite what some may claim. It's been around since the 15th century, and while the last few years have seen a decline it's still the diamond capital of the world. Make no mistake about it. We were here long before New York, Hong Kong or Hatton Garden came about and got in on the business. Amsterdam had its run for a while," Toby shifted uneasily at the sound of the name of the city they stole the goods from, "But it's not Antwerp – 80% of the world's rough diamonds are traded here. Around 50% of the world's polished diamonds are traded here. Approximately 1850 registered diamond businesses have their offices right here in the Square Mile. The Indians might be undercutting us, sure," he shrugged, "but they'll never have our knowledge, connections and class. How could they? No, precision cutting has always been our specialty and the machines just don't do it the same elsewhere." He shook his head. "Not to a trained eye like mine. Legacy, infrastructure, expertise, geographical location... we have it all here and what do the Indians have?" He stopped looking through the magnifier to stare at Mark and Toby for an answer to what was really a rhetorical question.

"Curry and a fetish for gang rape on public transport?" Toby eventually asked, looking at Mark for confirmation but he just hung his head in disbelief at Toby's lack of charm, style or shame.

"Cheap labour," the jeweller said, also unimpressed with Toby's answer. "And, as the saying goes, 'you get what you pay for.'"

"So what will you pay us for these?" Mark asked quickly. He was very bored with the Wikipedia-style article being told by the arrogant fat man and wanted to nip things in the bud before his friend made anymore racist comments. Mark knew that Toby wasn't actually racist, he just had a habit of saying ignorant shit.

The jeweller was not happy with being cut off, "Do you have certification for any of the diamonds? HRD or even GIA?"

"WTF?" Toby blurted out.

The fat man removed his gloves and reclined in the chair. He studied the pair of ignorant salesmen for a moment and then sighed. "What are you after boys?"

"Money, obviously," Toby said.

"Frankly, you'd stand a better chance with masks and guns."

"What?" Mark knew haggling when he heard it and also started to think that Jewish people had the reputation they have for a reason.

"This stuff is garbage," the fat man said spreading his arms to indicate the stolen goods. "There's not a decent piece in your whole collection. I know I said 80% of the world's rough diamonds come here, but rough is an understatement for what you have."

"I'm pretty sure there's some top-quality gear there in front of you. Haggling is all well and good, but at least be civilised about it." Mark let the jeweller know that he had a limit to how far he would let the fat man go with his bartering.

The jeweller smiled and nodded. "I tell you what boys," he said in a friendly tone, "leave your bag with me. I'll have my people go through it properly, check everything thoroughly and then you come back tomorrow and I make you an offer." He spread his arms again and looked at each seller, "How does that sound?"

"You expect us to just leave everything with you and you give us—"

"A receipt," the jeweller cut Toby off. "As is done by all professional businesses young man."

Toby looked at Mark, not sure what to say, do or think. Mark leaned forwards and extended a hand for the fat man to shake with a warm smile to accompany it, "Deal."

The jeweller shook Mark's hand and returned the smile while asking "You have the number for your hotel? I will call you tomorrow when we have finished."

"Actually," Mark kept the fake smile plastered across his dirty face, "we haven't picked one yet. Maybe you can give us your card and we'll call you early afternoon. How does that sound?"

"Good," the jeweller replied as he handed Mark his business card   from   off   his   desk.

Even with the car seats reclined they couldn't really get comfortable. They'd found a space on a street leading out of the centre that didn't require any payment for parking and decided it was as good a place as any to hole up for the night. Toby had complained for a while about the lack of weed or any other substances, before Mark had finally had to tell him to shut up and try to get some rest. Both of their minds refused to stay silent despite being exhausted from the drive and the adventure.

When they had managed to avoid going to prison in the UK there was a destination and a goal in mind. It had been Toby's dream for many years and Mark was happy to share in it: a coffee shop in Amsterdam. But now there was no end in sight. They didn't even have a country to call home, yet alone a plan to implement once they were there. Returning to the UK was suicide in their minds. They truly felt lost. Mark was fine with taking each day as it came for the time being but Toby couldn't let the subject lie.

"Let's say we do get some decent scratch for the stones," it wasn't long before Toby broke the silence again. "What comes next?"

"No idea," Mark groaned, with his eyes still closed and mind set on sleep.

"Amsterdam had always been the dream and now that's gone..." Toby trailed off, sounding and feeling more depressed than ever. They sat in silence in the darkness for a few minutes before Toby yet again opened his mouth. "How about America?"

"What about America?"

"We could try our luck there," Toby perked up at the idea. "Huge drugs market. Land of opportunity and all that."

"Lot of competition," Mark sighed. "No contacts," his mind filled with arguments against the suggestion without even giving it any real thought. "Long fucking distance to travel."

"We could go to Memphis. You could—"

"Go to sleep Toby."

Again, the car was filled with a silence that both Mark and Toby knew would be short-lived. The pair both understood that some kind of plan for the future was needed. It didn't need to be a long-term idea, but certainly something beyond collecting the cash for the stolen jewellery. Mark was happy to leave the subject until he'd rested and was in a better frame of mind to concoct some clear and rational thoughts. On the other hand Toby wanted something to occupy his mind that seemed unable to switch off without some form of intoxicant.

"We need a game plan dude," the cook insisted.

"Let's see what happens tomorrow first." Mark sighed and tried to turn his back on Toby. For all they knew the jeweller could change his mind and not give them anything for the stolen goods. For all they knew he could offer them very little. As far as Mark was concerned, plans were pointless until after they had some cash in their hand.

Toby nodded silently while his mind raced for other alternatives to the US. *Surely Mandarin can't be that hard to master...*

To their surprise, the fat jeweller was waiting at the back of the store for them with a large warm smile and outstretched hands with fingers covered in stones and precious metals.

Mark and Toby sleepily strolled through the ground floor and half-smiled at the jeweller and his two heavyset security guards. Even though the men were dressed in dark suits that fitted them perfectly, it was obvious they were the shop security and not customers or gemologists. They kept faces of sullen stone while their boss smiled like a man about to make a mint.

"Boys, boys, boys: I have good news for you," said the squat man who welcomed Mark and Toby like long-lost sons. "I know someone who is very interested in the items you brought me. Come, this way," he continued as he led the pair of amateurs towards a back room. "Let me do the talking here boys and we'll get the best sale possible, yes?" he said as he looked over his shoulder at the confused thieves.

"And I suppose there's a nice fat fee in there somewhere for you too," Toby said the obvious as they all entered a short and narrow bare concrete corridor that led to what looked like a fire escape with two figures standing before it.

Mark then realised that the jeweller's two security guards were no longer walking behind them and had stopped to lock and stand in the way of the door they'd just walked through. His half-asleep brain started to put pieces into place that he hoped were all wrong.

"This is how business works young man," the jeweller continued as they approached the other two men. "You've heard of a finder's fee surely, yes?" The men who stood before the one and only exit out of the corridor were now clearly visible. They were two monoliths dressed in black from head to toe in what looked more like tech wear than suits or typical garb found in the Diamond Quarter. "Here you are boys, these are the men who are interested in what you have to sell." The jeweller's tone had changed now and he looked down at his feet and not at Mark and Toby or the so-called buyers.

"I'm not seeing much in the way of cash and we ain't accepting Luncheon Vouchers," Toby opened negotiations, "or any other bull—"

"How about lead?" one of the strangers asked as the pair of them quickly took pistols out and aimed them at Mark and Toby. Both guns had silencers on them and were held with steady hands.

"Shit," Toby said defeated and now 100% sure that they had been fucked by the short fat man.

"You're gonna fucking rob us?" Mark asked.

"Actually, these men work for the man who *you* robbed," the jeweller brought Mark and Toby up to speed. "We don't take kindly to thieves in this business, and we all watch each other's backs." The fat man now smiled cunningly at the witless duo.

One of the shooters took thick plastic restraints from a pocket and held them out for Mark and Toby to see. "Turn around slowly," he instructed them with an English accent and an authoritative tone. "Hands behind your backs, fingers interlinked and don't start no shit." His eyes hardened as he almost dared the pair to disobey him.

Mark and Toby sighed as they did what was asked of them. As soon as the plastic cuffs were around their wrists and tightened to the point of cutting off their blood supply to their hands, everything went black for Mark as one of the men asked him, "Tell me, does this smell of chloroform?"

Toby just caught a glimpse of one of the men smothering his partner-in-crime with a rag before the same happened to him.

Darkness smothered the pair of outlaws.

Mark drifted down into the dark at first, but found that his speed picked up by the force pushing up against him. There was just the pitch black nothingness at first with the sensation of falling. He was aware of himself but saw nothing. He heard only the sound of the air passing by his free-falling self that got louder and louder as a further indication of how fast he was falling.

And then light appeared.

It came from above, like a spotlight aimed at his back from somewhere up on high in the nothingness. He could partially see himself, but beyond it everything was a blank – just the endless blackness. He was able to keep his eyes open as he fell into the void because they were protected by his trusty old sunglasses, the thought of which brought with it the feeling of another presence there with him in the big black.

"Long time no see," Mark said with a smirk and paused before uttering the word, "Hoss."

"Did you miss me?" a cocksure and familiar voice asked with that unforgettable Southern drawl. "I bet you did."

Drifting towards Mark as he fell he saw a reflection of his own gold sunglasses out of the darkness. Then came the face followed by a body wrapped in a black leather jump-suit. The pair fell and smiled at each other, illuminated from above by the unseen spotlight that increased the diameter of its beam to include Elvis.

"Where you headed?" asked the King of Rock 'n' Roll with eyebrows raised high above the gold frames.

Mark looked straight down into the bottomless depths with a smile, all the while thinking about the answer to that question. After a moment he arched his head back to look at his companion in free fall, "Straight down. All the way down."

"I like your style," smiled Elvis. "Hey Mark, shouldn't you have a parachute for a fall like this?"

"Did you ever have one?"

"Here," Elvis suddenly extended his hand towards Mark and offered him something wrapped in paper, "have a cheeseburger. They're delicious, I swear."

Mark smiled as he reached for the food and then suddenly felt the   impact   of   the   fall.

Smoke like he'd never witnessed before. So thick it was like standing in candy floss and to Toby it was just as sweet smelling and tempting. While it wasn't pink in colour, it certainly smelt and tasted like it ought to be.

Saliva cascaded from Toby's partially open jaw as he shuffled blindly through the indica fog that he found himself in. Where he was and where he was going mattered not, it was like a strange heaven where the air itself got you high with the most incredible of flavours. Toby's eyes filled with tears at the beauty of it all. There were no words for how incredible he felt.

He continued to casually drift through the pungent aroma when just as strangely it began to disappear. The cook started to panic and tried to scoop as much of the smoke into his open mouth as he could while running around the greyness like a man possessed.

Then it was all gone and Toby found himself standing in the ruins of a demolished building. It didn't appear familiar at first, and then he stepped further into it and realised he was walking through the remnants of what was once The Atom Café. Again, Toby's eyes began to fill with water but for a different reason this time. He sifted through the debris and picked up pieces of still-smouldering furniture and apparatus. The smell of burned wood and toxic chemicals now replaced the sweet smoke that had preceded it.

Suddenly he heard them and felt their auras there in the bombsite with him. He turned, his eyes darting all around to find them but couldn't see anything. He charged through the ashes and dust, pushing aside what was left of the furniture that had survived the blast. They were watching him and he knew it.

From above him he heard them more clearly.

Not breathing.

Not speaking.

They were sniggering.

Toby slowly arched his neck back and tilted his head up to look straight into the big black eyes of those two most curious of creatures. His heart stopped for a moment and then beat faster and faster until it felt like it was going to punch straight out through his ribcage and escape Europe altogether.

The rabbits stared down at him and continued to chuckle scornfully. The chuckle turned into laughter, which in turn increased in volume and pitch to a half-banshee-like scream and half-cackle of deliriousness.

Toby screamed in terror right before the rabbits hopped off their perches high above him to fall wide-eyed and screaming with shards of what appeared to be glass gripped tightly in their white fluffy paws. Toby's hands sprang up defensively before his face with eyes now shut tight to somehow shield him from the horror of what he was seeing and the inevitable pain of the stabbing.

Waking from an unexpected sleep can be very disorientating. Waking from that sleep while standing up only adds to the bizarre feeling. When the first thing you see is your oldest friend staring right back at you with wide and terrified eyes your testicles react by violently contracting. Add to that the tight and constricting feeling of plastic around your wrists, which are secured behind you, and the almost as tight sensation of cotton fibres around your neck and there are many who would believe it justifiable to panic.

This is why the voice was quick to say, "Don't panic. Don't move. Just concentrate on breathing."

Mark realised the voice belonged to one of the men who had kidnapped them at the jewellers. The man kitted out in all black was now stood before him just a few feet below. Toby stared bug-eyed at his side, but it made breathing too difficult to keep looking at his friend so he looked straight ahead and took in the surroundings in his peripheral.

It was the smell that he noticed first though. Before the mud, hay and corrugated iron that made up the housing of the structure they were in there was the all-pervasive smell of faeces. Swine shit has a very foul and fetid stink. The accompanying squeals and snorts behind him further confirmed they were on a pig farm. He had a sideways glance at his partner who stood on the tips of his toes on a metal drum to ease the flow of oxygen being cut off by the noose around his neck, which hung from a rafter above them.

The pair of former drug dealers balanced at the centre of the pigsty with thick ropes around their throats immediately knew that this was the end of their debauched and hedonistic lives. They had no idea who the pair of strangers dressed in black were but they worked for someone powerful who wanted them dead, that much was clear. The reason for wanting to hang them was the stolen jewels, they remembered that much. Both Mark and Toby were conscious enough to realise that there was a long list of possible suspects who would like to see them dead. From The French Connection to The Grim Union biker gang and all the way back into their past to Dick's crew, the part-time bodybuilder, part-time business man and fulltime psychotic cunt who was the first to fall on that fateful day back in Wales. However, none of them owned jewellery stores in Amsterdam.

As Mark and Toby concentrated on standing as still as possible balanced on their toes so they could continue to get oxygen to their lungs, a third figure approached through the giant open front of their metal surroundings. The daylight silhouetted him until he was stood directly in front of them.

Toby had no idea who the new arrival was but Mark had seen him before. He still wore an immaculate suit and carried himself with a swagger that let you know at first glance that he was in charge.

The tanned and ageing bodybuilder dressed in a bespoke suit sporting expensive cufflinks looked odd with the giant Wellington boots on his feet. He grimaced up at the duo and then fixed a pair of dazzling green eyes on Mark.

"We've met before," said Mr Jameson with a sure smile.

"New house?" choked Mark, while he remembered the opulent glass structure in the Welsh countryside where he had first seen the man before him over a year ago. "Not gonna use that expensive pea-shooter I delivered to you?"

Mr Jameson took a step back while checking his Rolex. "Unfortunately I don't have the necessary time to enjoy hurting you both," he looked up at Mark and Toby, "but you stole from me. My name is Mr Jameson, owner of Jameson Jewels. Theft is not something I take lightly, despite the items you stole being of no real value or consequence to me." He then suddenly lunged forwards and kicked the barrel from beneath Toby. "So, I'll just take pleasure in watching the short time it takes for you to hang to your deaths before continuing with more pressing matters."

The cook's body thrashed around as the life was choked out of him. His one and only regret was that he would die sober. *Disgusting!*

Mark looked on in horror and his mind raced for a way out of his and Toby's impending doom. From an earlier life he remembered delivering a gun to a guy's insanely over-the-top glass castle deep in the countryside. He remembered the protesters that surrounded the gates. He remembered a photograph. He remembered the face. He recognised the eyes. He recognised the name and description of an untouchable killer with vast wealth at his disposal.

"I know where your son is!" screamed Mark as loud as he could at the perfectly styled hair directly beneath him.

Mr Jameson drew his foot back and away from the barrel holding Mark up and placed the rubber boot back down firmly in the mud. He took a moment before looking up into Mark's eyes. "What did you say?"

"Your son, Paul," Mark glanced over at Toby, who was now taking his final look at the world around him through bloodshot eyes that bulged like balloons about to pop. "Help Toby and I'll tell you everything!"

Mr Jameson took another moment to think and then lifted the barrel below Toby and placed it where his feet could just reach the top.

Toby wretched, gasped and inhaled as hard as he could, his eyes bulging out of his face and drool staining his mangy beard. He hadn't heard what his friend had said to save his life, but he was grateful.

"Speak," commanded Mr Jameson. He stayed to the side of Toby's legs with his hand gripping the rim of the barrel tightly.

"He's in Europe. He left us in France," Mark cried out hoarsely. "Cut us down and I'll give you more specific details."

Mr Jameson stepped forwards and then his head exploded in an eruption of crimson. His custom threads dropped into the mud and pig shit as his dead body collapsed, minus his coiffed head.

Before the two kidnappers could react, two more shots rang out in quick succession and put them on the ground, again missing their heads.

Mark and Toby both tried to spot the shooter while waiting for their bullets to hit them and end their lives next. But nothing came. No gunshots. No pain. No blood. Just the sounds of swine feasting somewhere below them. They tried to struggle against the cable ties around their wrists to no avail. Occasionally they would glance at each other and then regret seeing themselves in identical situations.

"Well, I couldn't have planned this better if I'd tried," a familiar voice spoke from the entrance to the pigsty.

Mark and Toby stopped struggling with their restraints. The voice had finally caught up with them. *How in the fuck did he find us?* was on both of their minds, along with an increasing cold creeping sensation of fear as they squinted at the approaching figure of The French Connection.

Their former taskmaster strolled towards them, rifle in one hand and cigarette in the other. The bastard almost smiled as he looked at the pair of idiots who had caused him so much trouble.

"I won't deny it boys, you lost me for a time there," TFC said as he stood casually before Mark and Toby. "But I found you. I knew it would only be a matter of time until you fucked up and landed right back in my hands."

"How's about letting us down for old times' sake, hey boss?" Toby managed to force the words from between his swollen lips. He hated the bastard, but at least they had had a profitable past together at one time. *Maybe TFC could just give us another shit job to do*, he thought.

TFC smiled up at him as he kicked the barrel out from beneath the cook, "With pleasure."

For the second time, Toby dangled like a marionette being controlled by an unruly child. Only this time there was nothing Mark could say or do to help him.

Toby choked his last and stared into the vacant black eyes of the two long-eared figures that waited for him silhouetted by the setting sun.

"Any last words?" TFC grimaced up at Mark.

"Fuck yo—"

Made in the USA
Coppell, TX
18 December 2023

25608205R00115